Sin

A BROTHER'S BEST FRIEND COLLEGE ROMANCE

PURITY
BOOK FOUR

SKYLER MASON

To my Lord and Savior (of this book) Claire Taylor. Just as Lazarus was raised from the dead, you resurrected my belief in myself and breathed new life into my writing.

Chapter One

Lily

Night should be my enemy. It's when I made my worst mistake.

It's so damn beautiful though. The ocean fog wraps the world in an ethereal haze, and the moonlight shimmers on the dew-soaked grass. What mixture of colors would capture that silvery-purple sparkle? No less than five different paints would do them justice.

How could the world feel so welcoming—so full of mystical possibilities—when my life is unraveling? For the moment, my heart is quiet. Once I enter the sorority house and go up into the bedroom where it all happened six months ago, this peace will vanish into the night. My brain will start humming, growing louder and more frantic until morning finally comes.

I hate that cursed room. I wish I never had to sleep in it again.

I creep toward the side of the house, humiliation clawing at my skin. I'm about to crawl through the window like a thief, just to avoid scrutiny.

I don't want my sisters to know that I'm out again on a school night. They've all been worried about me, especially Kinsley, our sorority mother hen. Apparently, I've been "quiet" and "not myself" recently.

I wish I could pretend that I was out at a party or at a friend's house—like the old Lily would have been—but I don't have the energy to lie. The truth is I've been walking the neighborhood streets of Santa Barbara all alone, hoping to exhaust my brain enough to make it stop spinning.

I *am* exhausted—bone-deep weary—but I doubt it will help me sleep. I can't seem to calm my brain after what Mason did to me.

With utmost care, I edge closer to my window, my heart thumping against my ribcage. I cracked it open before I left for my walk just for this moment. The cold metal frame is like ice against my fingertips thanks to the ocean moisture.

Footsteps thump behind me, sending a chill down my spine. When I whip around, a tall, broad-shouldered form looms in the darkness.

"Did you walk home alone?" asks a deep voice.

Goddamn it.

Ethan Harrington. My older brother's best friend, and more recently, my nemesis. He's always been a pain in my ass, but it's become much more frequent now that my bedroom window faces his. This isn't the first time he's caught me sneaking home late, though never through my window.

How fucking embarrassing.

"Ethan, if I'd screamed, I could have woken up my whole sorority." I glance over his shoulder at the Victorian mansion behind him. "Your frat brothers, too."

He takes a step forward, and the dim lantern casts warm, golden light over his face. God, he's gorgeous with his strong jaw and wavy hair that's now tousled from sleep. His thick arms stretch the fabric of his T-shirt, revealing a body sculpted by strength and endurance.

He doesn't look like this because he spends hours lifting weights out of vanity, like so many gym rats I know. Ethan's physique has been honed by hours of hard work on the field. As the star wide receiver on the Mission Valley Hawks, he uses his body as a tool.

Somehow, that makes him so much hotter.

Heat creeps into my cheeks. Where the hell are these horny thoughts coming from? I must be exhausted. Ethan's athleticism has never turned me on before. It's a sign of how all he ever does is work. He wouldn't recognize fun if it gave him a lap dance. All he cares about is football and God, like the perfect golden boy he is.

"Answer my question," Ethan says. "Did you walk all the way home from the bars by yourself?"

He always assumes my late-night wandering is a trip home from the bars, because that's exactly what the old Lily would be doing. Ethan clocked me as reckless and immature the moment my brother, Noah, introduced us during my first week at Mission Hills University over two years ago.

In those early months of freshman year, I spent too much time with him and Noah—following them to parties and joining their group hangouts. It didn't take long for me to find my own group of friends, but those first few months of following Noah around must have left a lasting impression on Ethan.

He can't stand me, and he makes it brazenly obvious whenever I'm in his presence.

"I stayed on well-lit streets," I say.

He shakes his head. "Stupid."

His high-handedness sparks a fire within me. My first pleasant feeling since I started creeping around my own house like a criminal. Good boy Ethan thinks I'm much wilder than I really am, and one of my favorite ways to tease him is to lean into his misconception.

I shoot him a cheeky smile. "I needed to walk off my soreness. I just left an orgy. They were big guys, too. Very well-endowed." I gesture with my hands a penis size far too large for any human man.

Ethan's eyelids flutter closed, and he inhales a shaky breath, as if he's straining for control. "If they were *that* well-endowed, I'm surprised you're still in one piece."

I suck in my lips to fight a smile. I wasn't expecting him to play along with me. "They had to warm me up first," I say. "Lots of foreplay and—"

"Okay." He lifts a hand. "No more about your non-existent orgy. I don't need to know where you were, but you do need to stop doing this. Promise me in the future, you won't walk home alone at night."

I let out a long sigh. I can't make a promise like that. Wandering the streets at night is the only thing that stops my brain from buzzing. It might not exhaust me enough to sleep, but it's far more pleasant than lying restlessly in that bed.

"No, I can't," I say firmly.

Ethan's jaw clenches. "Then how about you stop partying on weeknights? I already know..." His lips purse. "Noah told me you've been struggling in school lately."

A wave of irritation ripples over my skin. I know that Noah has been worried about me since my grades started dropping, but how dare he talk to Ethan about it?

Ethan is the last person in the world I want to see my struggles. He's too damn perfect—a star athlete with excellent grades, and most annoying of all, a devout Christian who made a chastity pledge. Practically a celebrity on campus, he has hundreds of women throwing themselves at him, but he's saving himself for his future wife, whoever she might be. His perfect, gorgeous, and chaste future wife. A woman who would never date a man like Mason. Never let a man like him come into her bedroom and...

I'm spiraling. I did nothing wrong that night. And why the hell am I comparing myself to Ethan's faceless future wife? She'll be boring and straitlaced, just like him. I don't envy her at all. All his gorgeousness can't make up for how insufferable he is .

I let out a sigh. "Of course you brought up my bad grades. You're my reliable joy vacuum. You saw me coming home and figured I had a wild night. So you had to rush out here and suck up all the good vibes before I go to bed."

Ethan stares at me, his eyes locking onto mine. There's a flicker of something in his gaze, and the corners of his mouth twitch, as if he's fighting to keep a straight face.

My God, is Ethan holding back laughter? How unlike him. He generally rolls his eyes at the numerous nicknames I've called him over the years.

"Your joy vacuum," he mutters almost to himself. "I like that better than Grumplestiltskin. It's almost...poetically mean. Like you spent hours trying to figure out the biggest insecurity of an overachiever like me, and once you figured it out, you went straight for the heart."

My skin prickles. Insecurity? Ethan doesn't understand the meaning of the word. Self-doubt doesn't exist in his world. Confidence is his default setting, because life has never given him a reason to feel otherwise.

"I wasn't trying to be mean," I say, softening my voice. "I'm just tired of being reminded about my grades. I get it enough from Noah."

Ethan takes a step in my direction. "He's worried about you. I am too."

I snort. "Don't pretend like you care about me. You just enjoy bossing me around."

"When have I ever..." He shuts his eyes, inhaling a shaky breath. He can't even try to refute what I said, because he's too principled to tell a lie.

Ethan *is* bossy. He's even more overbearing and protective than Noah. Over the years, whenever we've been at the same party —which is often since we're both in the Greek scene—Ethan has inevitably stepped in and ruined my fun, especially when I'm with guys.

It's like he has a sixth sense for when I'm starting to enjoy myself. I'll be talking to someone, maybe even flirting a little, and then suddenly, there he is, his presence a dark cloud over my evening.

"I'm sorry if I haven't been good at showing it," Ethan says, "but I do care about you."

Right. He cares about me the way he would a distant family member he can't stand.

Ethan's gaze flickers over my shoulder. "Were you planning to climb through the window?"

My skin prickles. "I don't want to wake the house."

His eyes narrow. "I see lights on. I don't think they're all asleep."

How can I explain my behavior? I hardly understand it myself. Why do I need to keep it a secret that I stay out late every night? My sorority sisters can't see the turmoil inside me. Just because I've been acting differently lately doesn't mean they'll jump to the conclusion that I'm broken inside.

I'm *not* broken inside, and yet I want to hide.

"I've been stressed lately," I say. "I go out at night to clear my head. I'd rather not have the whole house know my business."

He scoffs. "You're stressed out about your grades, so you deal with it by partying. Great way to cope. You'll be off academic probation in no time."

Heat rushes through my veins, making my jaw clench. How dare he judge me when he has no idea what I've been through?

"Great talk, Ethan," I clip out. "I feel so much better. Really energized to turn my grades around. Now please leave." I point to his frat house.

His stern expression falters. "I'm sorry. I shouldn't have said that. It was...judgmental."

I shrug. "It's okay. Making me feel bad is your one job as my joy vacuum. Well, you've succeeded. I feel like shit. You can go now."

His face falls. "I really wasn't trying to make you feel like shit. I'm sorry."

I wave a hand. "Then make me feel better by leaving."

He stares at me for a long moment. "I'm not leaving until I know you're safe inside that house."

I laugh humorlessly. Just what I need. Ethan watching me clumsily hoisting myself through that window. As if I'm not embarrassed enough for planning to climb through it in the first place.

"No," I say. "I want you to leave."

His eyes grow hesitant for a moment—just a flash—but then he takes a few steps back and onto the side yard of the frat house. "I'm just getting some air," he says with a smirk. "Carry on with your business."

I roll my eyes dramatically. Fuck, he's the worst. So smug and self-righteous. He thinks it's his duty as Noah's best friend to make sure I'm safe, and he doesn't give a damn about my feelings.

In a snap decision, I march forward until I'm inches away from him. His head jerks back in surprise, but I don't let it deter me. I grab his shoulders and shove him in the direction of the front porch of his frat house. He doesn't budge, so I press harder, to no avail. "Go. Now."

His dark-blue eyes grow huge. "What the hell are you doing?"

"I want you to leave."

"Why do you even care if I watch you go inside? I already know you're planning to crawl through the window."

I keep pressing against his shoulders, but he stands firm. When I use all my body weight to shove him, my feet slide back on the damp lawn. Damn, he's built like an ox.

"You're acting insane," he says. "Calm down."

Insane. Calm down. Such simple words, and yet they hit me in the chest like hailstones. Didn't Mason say something similar the morning after it all happened?

"You're acting crazy, Lily," he'd said.

I lift a hand high in the air, aiming it in the direction of Ethan's face.

His eyes grow impossibly huge as he grabs my wrist. "What the hell is wrong with you?"

"I hate you," I say through clenched teeth.

Except I don't hate him. Why am I taking my rage against Mason out on Ethan? Is it because Mason is Ethan's teammate and Noah's roommate? Do I subconsciously blame them for not knowing the truth about him?

Crazy. I haven't told anyone what he did for a reason. I want to forget it all.

Ethan's eyes flash as he grips my wrist tighter. "You hate me because I want to make sure you're safe?"

I raise my chin, searching my brain for any excuse to explain my odd behavior. "You want to watch me crawl through that window so you can delight in how perfect your life is compared to mine."

Anger fills his eyes. Shit, I must have hit a nerve, and I wasn't even trying to.

Ethan yanks me against his hard chest, sending a jolt of shock through my veins. The air between us changes in an instant, crackling with electricity. His eyes settle on my mouth.

My head grows fuzzy. What is happening?

The thumping of his heart pulses against my chest, and my anger evaporates into the night. The warmth and hardness of his body makes heat pool in my belly.

No. I'm not attracted to Ethan. He's not attracted to me. We can't stand each other.

Then why are his eyes glazed and hooded as he stares at my mouth, like he's been drugged?

"Lily," he mutters before crashing his lips against mine.

Chapter Two

L^{ily}

His lips are hard at first, but then they soften. He nibbles on my mouth before letting out a groan. The delicious sound of it vibrates through my bones.

Am I dreaming?

I was ready to hit him moments ago. Now, he's kissing me, and this isn't just any kiss… It's hungry, almost desperate. He rubs his tongue against the seam of my mouth, begging for entrance.

A deep, distant voice tells me I'll regret kissing him back, but I open my mouth as if in a trance. He immediately slips his tongue inside, and sparks shoot through my belly. I let out a whimper. He must like the sound, because he grinds his hips against mine.

As our tongues dance together, his heart thumps against my chest like a steady drumbeat. I lift my hands to his head and run my fingers through his soft hair.

"Oh God, Lily," he murmurs against my lips.

I hum in response, and his whole body freezes.

I crash down to earth. What am I doing kissing Ethan? I haven't been able to stomach a man's touch since that night six months ago.

Ethan grabs my shoulders and pushes me back. His eyes are wide and glazed, as if he can't even comprehend the sight in front of him. He stares at me for what feels like an eternity before he opens his mouth. "Oh, shit."

If I weren't so dazed, I would probably laugh at his obvious shock. When have I ever seen unflappable Ethan Harrington this rattled?

"I have no idea why that just happened," he says quietly.

I scowl at his word choice. "That kiss didn't *just happen*. You initiated it."

He flinches. "I know."

I shake my head, my thoughts growing fuzzy. "Why? A second ago, you called me insane. I think that *kiss* was pretty insane."

He shuts his eyes and inhales a shaky breath. "It was, and I'm sorry. I never should have done it. It was...wrong."

Wrong. The word doesn't sit well with me. Wrong is what Mason did to me. Ethan's kiss was something else... Something I'd worried I'd never feel again. My body had burst into flames when he pressed his lips against mine. It's obnoxious to hear him dismiss it like the kiss was something dirty.

I smile lazily, not wanting him to see how unsettled I am. "You're a really good kisser. It's kind of shocking. Are you lying about the whole virgin thing? Maybe it's part of your game. You want to seem difficult to attain, a conquest for women."

His eyes alight, and his lips quirk. It sends a tingle over my skin. Since when does he like it when I tease him?

"Yeah, I pretend to be a virgin," he says, "because most women find that really sexy in a grown-ass man."

I cock a brow. "They would with you. Have you ever looked in a mirror?"

When his eyes grow wide, my cheeks heat. What am I doing

praising him like a groupie? That kiss must have messed with my head.

Ethan lowers his chin, his lips lifting into a devilish smile. "Are you trying to tell me I'm handsome, Lily?"

I roll my eyes. "You know you are. It's a shame you have such an insufferable personality. What a waste of a beautiful face."

He snorts. "God, you're vicious. So small and yet so fierce, like a little bobcat."

A giggle escapes my chest. "Bobcat. Noah would love that. I literally scratched his face when we were kids when he took my..."

His stricken expression makes me pause. "What's wrong?" I ask.

Ethan lifts a hand and rakes it through his hair. "Please don't tell Noah about what happened between us. He wouldn't... This was a freak thing, okay? I'm never going to kiss you again."

My skin heats. Is he implying that I want him to kiss me again?

God, he's so full of himself.

I scowl. "I'd never tell Noah about our kiss. No matter what I said, he'd think I seduced you. He was pissed at me for dating Mason. He has that stupid rule that I'm not allowed to date his teammates."

Ethan's expression softens. "He was more pissed at Mason than you. He's protective of you, and he doesn't want to cause any unnecessary strain on our team."

I cringe. "It's gross and misogynistic that he thinks he has a say over who I date just because I'm his little sister."

Ethan narrows his eyes. "And yet he was right to be worried about our team. He and Mason can barely stand each other. That's our quarterback. It's a big deal when the guy calling the shots can't get along with his teammates."

The idea of Mason being so exalted makes my skin crawl. He might be the quarterback, but he's not very good at it, at least according to Noah. The only reason why the Hawks are a big deal —garnering national attention—is because of Ethan.

I open my mouth to speak but freeze when a light goes on behind me. I turn around, and sure enough, the glow is coming from my window.

"Fuck," I mutter. "I think someone is checking on me."

Ethan shuffles his feet. "Alright get inside. I won't stick around to watch you crawl through the window. But I'd better not see you still out here by the time I get back to my room."

I roll my eyes. "There's no need to crawl through my window anymore. Someone is obviously waiting for me in my room."

His intense gaze is on my face. "Promise me you won't walk alone at night, Lily. I'm not asking because... I'm not trying to be a prick. I want to make sure you're safe."

Something about the look in his eyes and the warmth in his voice tells me he's sincere. Before tonight, I never would have thought Ethan gave a shit about me, but after that kiss, I'm not sure if I ever really understood him.

"I'll think about it," I say. "I can promise I won't go anywhere else tonight. Is that enough for you?

His expression grows hesitant. He stares at me for a long moment. "I guess it'll have to be."

My stomach fluttering, I turn around and walk in the direction of our porch. What a bizarre night.

My brother's best friend just kissed me, and I don't have a clue why he did it. Does annoyance make him horny? If so, he could have kissed me a million times before. I always aim to annoy Ethan.

When I open the front door to the house, Lorelai is sitting on the living room couch. She glances up from her textbook. "Kinsley is worried about you." Her voice is raspy, as if from disuse. "You should probably find her before she calls your brother."

I roll my eyes as I rush to my bedroom. Kinsley is a fierce caretaker, like it's her one mission in the world. It was only mildly annoying before my life turned upside down. Now, I can't stand her scrutiny. She knows something is off with me, and she won't leave me alone until I tell her.

She'll be waiting a long time. I don't owe anyone explanations.

I walk through the end of the hallway to my bedroom door. Before I push it open, I hesitate.

God, I hate this room. It taught me that vibes are a real thing. This whole house used to be full of golden light and warm energy. Now, my room is a cavern of shadows and tension, a prison cell of my unescapable anxiety.

When I open the door, Kinsley is sitting on my bed, thankfully here to distract me from my unpleasant thoughts. Her head jerks up when I enter. "You said you'd be home by midnight."

I shrug. "I felt like staying out later."

"It's almost three in the morning. On a school night."

I smile tightly. "Yes, mommie dearest. It is."

She lets out a heavy breath. "I'm not trying to be annoying. You can stay out as late as you want. I was just worried."

Tension eases from my body. Kinsley really does care, and it's not fair for me to be so irritated with her. She and I used to talk, and I haven't confided in her about anything since that night with Mason.

"I thought I heard your voice outside," Kinsley says. "Were you out with someone else?"

I open my mouth and then close it, wondering how much I should tell her about Ethan.

My jaw clenches. I won't say anything about the kiss, but I refuse to be his dirty little secret. He was acting like an ass tonight, and I have the right to vent about it.

It'll be good. It'll distract her from asking where I was tonight.

I smirk. "My lord and master was also worried when I came home so late, but he wasn't nearly as understanding as you."

A grin spreads over her face. "Ethan?"

"Yes."

She giggles. "Lily, he's obsessed with you."

She's said things like this before, and my stomach never fluttered like it is right now. Until that kiss, Kinsley's words had no merit in my eyes.

Ethan isn't obsessed with me, but after that kiss, I wonder if his irritation with me is more complicated.

I shake my head. "He's just protective of me, like a big brother. Noah is more than enough. I don't need another one."

She raises her brows. "Oh, you think that's why he's always hovering over you? Trust me, it's so much more than that. Every single girl in our church has gone after him at some point. He barely even looks their way. Yet when you're around, he's hyper focused and...electrified."

My stomach does a little turn. "What do you mean electrified?"

"I mean, he looks so calm and almost bored most of the time, but the second Lily Greenwood walks into a room, he lights up."

I wave a hand. "That's what he looks like when he's pissed off. It's hard to tell with Ethan, because he doesn't have a personality."

She shakes her head. "You're so mean to him, and I think he's into it. You know how they say the opposite of love isn't hate but indifference. And Ethan is *far* from indifferent to you."

I'd never give her words a second thought if it weren't for the kiss tonight. In one moment, his dark-blue eyes were blazing with anger. Then he pulled me against his chest, and the anger was gone in a flash. He looked ready to eat me.

I thought Ethan was as simple and straightforward as every all-American golden boy. Turns out I don't really know what's going on in that handsome head of his.

Chapter Three

E^{than}

I shove my practice jersey into my duffel bag with more force than necessary. I worked myself to death during the four-quarters drill. Punishment for my insane behavior last night.

I can still taste her mouth now... Sweet with a hint of mint. Soft and warm.

Delicious.

That small kiss had filled me with a need more potent than anything I've ever known. I wanted to bury myself inside her. Plunder her like a barbarian. My cock was as hard as a rock when I made it back to my bedroom.

What the hell is happening to me? I've only kissed two other women in my life, and never with as much abandoned intensity. I was so consumed by the pleasure, I don't think I remembered my own name, let alone my plan to stay pure until marriage.

The part that makes no sense is that I've never wanted Lily this way. She drives me insane.

Sure, I've had a few sexual thoughts about her over the years. Natural considering how beautiful she is with those bright-gray eyes and fiery-red hair. But I never indulge the fantasies. She's off-limits as Noah's little sister.

What would he think if he knew what I did last night? He hated Mason for pursuing Lily. Told him from the very beginning that he doesn't want his teammates dating his sister. It complicates things, he'd said. Creates strain on the team if the relationship goes sour.

I'm so much more than Noah's teammate. I'm his best friend. It ought to be a given that I'd never take advantage of his sister during a vulnerable moment.

And she was vulnerable last night. Even in her anger, I sensed something under the surface of her usual sass. She was troubled.

Instead of giving her comfort, I acted like a dick, refusing to leave when she'd asked me.

It was a mistake. That kiss never would have happened if I had just minded my damn business like she practically commanded me to do.

"Are you going to Devon's party tomorrow night?" Noah asks, pulling me out of my head.

"Probably not," I say, straining to keep my voice even. I don't want him to sense my guilt. "Being around a bunch of drunk people isn't as fun as it used to be."

He pulls his clean shirt over his head. "I don't know how it was ever fun. I can never be sober around drunk people. Your self-control is crazy." He smiles. "Probably why you're better at football than me."

I smirk. "Or maybe I'm more naturally talented."

"No way. I don't believe in that. That's fixed mindset. It's all about hard work."

He might be right. I've spent the last three years devoting myself to becoming better. Never slacking during practice. Keeping razor-sharp focus during games, which means getting plenty of sleep and spreading out my homework and studying throughout the week. I never cram.

Somehow, I've managed to keep a 3.8 GPA even with the distraction of football. My dream is to get into the NFL, but there are no guarantees. I'm not the most physically talented wide receiver. A stroke of luck last year determined my NFL potential. A scout happened to see me because he attended the game for another player.

God is calling me to be my best possible self. I know it, though I've never heard his voice directly. My fluke success in football has to be a sign of some kind. Though it might be a worldly pursuit, it'll put me in a position of influence, where I can do so much good in the world.

If only I felt like a better Christian now. I try so hard to make all the right choices, and yet I'm always falling short.

Like I did last night with Lily.

The murmur of conversations fade as Noah and I stride out of the locker room and into the dimming evening. Noah's phone rings over the sound of crunching gravel under our feet.

He takes one look at the screen before silencing the ring. "It's my mom. Probably calling me about something that could be answered in a single text."

I smile, though it takes effort. Acting normal with him is almost as grueling as the conditioning drills we just finished. "My mom does it too, but I look at it as just one thing off my to-do list. It saves me time. She expects at least one phone call a week."

He pats my back. "You have lists for everything. Weekly calls with your mom, workouts, your protein intake." He laughs. "Even your Bible reading and church attendance."

I snort. "It won't get done otherwise."

"I doubt that. You keep lists to prove to yourself how much your life is optimized."

The word "optimized" makes me want to cringe. Something about it feels so...lifeless. It implies a kind of sterile efficiency meant for machines.

Lily would love that, wouldn't she? *"It all makes sense, Ethan,"* she'd say if she were here right now. *"You have no personality because you're secretly a robot."*

A smile rises to my lips. I've never met anyone else who could tease me so mercilessly. I don't have a warm personality, and I'm a big guy. I assume that most people are at least a little intimidated by me. Not her. She's fearless, and it's fucking adorable.

"I wish Lily could take up list-making," Noah says, making me jump.

Holy shit, what am I doing thinking Lily is adorable? Sure, I'm attracted to her physically, but she's a menace. A giant pain in my ass. When she moved into the Alpha Theta Kappa house her sophomore year, Noah asked me to look out for her. I took that commitment seriously, and that girl is always out partying.

What is she doing, and who is she with, especially these last six months? I wish the thought didn't haunt me, but she's been so aloof and secretive. Is there some guy she's seeing that she doesn't want to tell anyone about? Maybe because he's older or married? My chest grows tight, and I clench my hands into fists at my side.

"Her grades are getting worse and worse," Noah says. "I don't think she's doing any studying."

I shrug. "She's probably going through something. She seems... I don't know, distant, I guess."

His dark eyes probe into mine. "You've noticed that too. I think something happened with Mason. Maybe... Do you think she was more into him than she let on, and their breakup really got to her?"

A prickling heat spreads over my skin. I can't stand the thought of Lily pining for Mason. I hated it when she started dating him, probably even more than Noah did. I could barely stomach seeing them together. Any time Mason had his hands on her, I wanted to yank him away from her.

I told myself it was because I'm protective of her, and Mason is a prick. A mediocre quarterback with a chip on his shoulder. He knows he's not NFL material, but it never seemed to bother him until I started excelling. Once I gained the attention of scouts, he started acting like a jealous, petty rival when we should be focused on winning games.

But somehow, after last night, that doesn't feel like the whole reason. Could I have some kind of repressed attraction to her? My older brother, Brandon, and his wife, Mariana, have been teasing me for years that I do, because I've complained about her so much.

If I do have some kind of twisted crush, it's not very strong. I've always had razor-sharp clarity about the things I want, and I don't want her. Even if she weren't off-limits.

"Fuck Mason," Noah says. "I knew he was into her, and I told him to stay away. Now look what happened. Lily barely talks to me, and he's acting like an even bigger dick to me than usual." He scoffs. "He's a dick to you, too. And you're the most important man on the team. We can't win without you."

I shrug. "He's a quarterback with a noodle arm who can't read a defense, so he wasn't helping me out much even before he started acting like a dick."

Noah grins, patting me on the back. "God, you're the best. I feel so much better about the fact that he slept with my sister." He winces. "I wish I hadn't said that. I don't even want to think about it."

I grit my teeth as my gut twists. I don't want to think about it either.

"Anyways," Noah says, "I'm not letting this Lily thing go. In fact, I'm planning an intervention."

I frown. "What do you mean an intervention?"

His jaw hardens. "I mean, she has to turn things around if she doesn't want to get kicked out of college. I was thinking of finding her an accountability partner. Kind of like a coach. Someone who can motivate her, help her set goals, and make sure she meets her deadlines."

My bafflement expands like a balloon. "You think Lily would agree to that?"

"Nope." His smile doesn't meet his eyes. "But I ran my plan by my parents, and they both agree with me that something drastic needs to happen. They said they won't pay her sorority dues next quarter if she doesn't turn her grades around. Tough love, you know? And they're putting me in charge."

I run my fingers through my hair, which is still damp from the shower. "Lily's not going to like that."

He scoffs. "Of course she won't, but it's for her own good."

"So you're going to become her accountability partner? I don't think—"

"No," he says, his gaze falling to the concrete. He shuffles his feet before lifting his head and meeting my eyes. Something about the look on his face makes the hairs on my arm stand up. "I think it needs to be you."

Anxiety grips my chest. "No."

His face falls. "Look, I know you're super busy, but I can't be the one to do this. She won't listen to me."

"She won't listen to me, either."

"She will. Once she gets over the fact that this is happening, she'll start listening. It can't be me. I'm too involved. Too frustrated with her to be objective. Besides, you're a way better student than me. She could really learn from you."

Why is my pulse hammering against my throat? I'm not going to do this.

I can't be around Lily more than I already am. Simply moving into my new room with a window facing hers has wreaked havoc on my equilibrium. Her presence draws my eyes like a magnet. Sometimes, I'll sense her nearby without hearing her voice or catching sight of that fiery red hair. My gaze drifts to the window, and there she is.

Besides, Noah wouldn't be asking me to do this if he knew I kissed her last night.

I should tell him. He wouldn't press me to become her accountability partner if he knew, and I can explain that the kiss was only a strange impulse, something I don't fully understand. As long as I keep my distance from her, it'll never happen again.

I open my mouth, but the words don't come.

I can't tell him.

He wouldn't even recognize me. I'm his steady, principled friend who plans to save himself for his future wife, a woman he hasn't even met yet. Noah knows I've only kissed two women in my whole life.

Noah takes a step closer, his expression growing grave. "This is a huge favor, and I'm not asking for it lightly. I'm…" He shuts his eyes. "I'm really worried about her."

My gut sinks like a stone. If I'm not going to tell him what happened, how can I say no? He doesn't ask favors of me very often, especially when they involve an extended time commitment. He knows how rigid I am about my routines.

He needs me.

And if I'm being honest with myself about my vow never to kiss Lily again, what is the danger in saying yes?

"I'll think about it," I say.

The smile that spreads over his face makes me want to wince. I haven't even agreed to it yet, but he knows me well. I'm not the type of person who raises the expectations of friends who need me, only to dash their hopes later. I'm as good as committed.

I'll have to be creative if I want to get out of this.

"Thank you," he says. "I really think you're the best person to help her." His lips quirk. "You're definitely the only straight man I'd trust not to come on to her. I guess it's a good thing you both can't stand each other."

I force a smile. *Can't stand her.* Even twenty-four hours ago, I would have heartily agreed with him. How could that kiss have changed everything?

Chapter Four

L^{ily}

I groan as I shove my phone into my messenger bag. "We need to talk" means "I'm going to scold you" in Noah's language.

I don't need this now, especially when this isn't even the worst text I received today. I got another one from Mason. Repeating his request to meet with me.

Sure, Mason. Let's go get a round of beers and reminisce about the night you...

My throat grows tight. I hate even thinking about it.

Anyway, I ghosted him as usual. If he wants to meet with me, it's probably only to repeat his threat that I can never tell anyone what I accused him of that morning.

When I make it to the steps of the sorority house, I halt, giving myself a moment before I go inside. I'm too fucking weary for this talk with my brother. I already know that my grades are bad. Extra pressure from Noah will only stress me out more.

After a few moments, I finally ascend the steps and walk inside. Two of my sorority sisters are standing in the living room. They turn to me with smiles on their faces. "Your brother's here," Ava says.

Lorelai grins. "With Ethan Harrington."

Anxiety prickles my skin, making me unable to tease Lorelai about her giddiness over Ethan. My sorority sisters are in awe of him—like he's a movie star—and I usually point out the absurdity of worshiping someone so self-righteous and boring.

I can't think of a single sassy thing to say. My head is swimming. Why the hell is Ethan here?

"Where are they?" I ask.

"I think they went to your room," Ava says. "Lorelai and I tried to make conversation, but Ethan wasn't having it." She wrinkles her nose. "I think he's in a grumpy mood."

"He's always like that," I say.

"Try to get them to come out here." Lorelai says. "I don't care if Ethan's grumpy. I'm getting a picture with him and sending it to my brother. He's a huge college football fan." She smiles mischievously. "I'm going to tell him I'm besties with Mr. Number Forty-Four."

When both girls laugh, I force a smile. My heart is pounding in my chest as I turn around and walk down the hallway.

Is it possible that Ethan told Noah about the kiss? It would be an incredibly strange thing to do, given that it's none of Noah's damn business, and Ethan specifically asked me not to tell him anything. But then again...

Ethan's strict morality makes him a strange guy. Maybe he had a change of heart about keeping the kiss a secret. I can't imagine it sits well with him to hide something from his best friend—especially when he knows it would piss Noah off.

The last time Noah came over to have a talk with me was months ago. It was when Mason first started pursuing me. Noah told me that his teammates were off-limits, that it could wreak havoc on their team dynamics if I got involved with one of them.

No matter how misogynistic and self-centered the request was, I wish I had listened.

When I make it to my bedroom door, it's ajar. I push it open and find Noah sitting at my desk and Ethan standing by my dresser and staring at my painting of my childhood dog, Barkley, that hovers above it.

"What is this about?" I ask, too irritated for greetings.

Noah lets a long sigh. "I had a talk with Mom and Dad over the weekend. We're all worried about your grades."

My stomach drops. I suspected this, but somehow the prospect of it feels even worse than being scolded for kissing his best friend. Does Noah think a lecture from him—on behalf of Mom and Dad—is going to motivate me to work harder?

"This is your second quarter on academic probation," Noah says. "If you don't turn this around, you could be kicked out of school by the end of the year. You only have one year left, Lily. You'd be throwing away almost three years of hard work and tuition."

My heart is in my throat. Does he think I don't know this?

"And why is Ethan here?" I ask.

Ethan looks at me for the first time since I walked into the room, his eyes unusually bright, emitting warmth that seems to reach across the space and wrap around me. "Did you paint this?" he asks, gesturing at Barkley's panting face.

I frown at the non-sequitur question. "No, I paid for a medi-ocre painting of a random golden retriever and hung it on my bedroom wall."

His lips quirk. "It's not mediocre. In fact, it's really good. It looks so..." He turns back to the painting. "It looks real."

Warmth washes over me at his compliment, even though the painting is pretty tepid for a student in her junior year of a Fine Arts program. Real is easy. Depth of feeling is what most art students find elusive.

Who cares about any of that? I need to know why the hell Noah invited Ethan to take part in a discussion about my falling grades.

"We've come up with a plan to help you," Noah says.

My head jerks in his direction. "My grades are none of your—"

"I need you to listen." Noah lifts a hand. "You can argue later. Your grades might not be my business, but they are Mom and Dad's. They pay your tuition."

I grit my teeth. How dare he team up with Mom and Dad to ambush me. He should be on *my* side. He's complained enough over the years about how often Mom and Dad have used their financial support to manipulate us. They wouldn't even let me major in art without a business administration minor—what they call a practical plan B for if the whole "art thing" doesn't pan out. Noah constantly complains about how often they remind him to make his studies a priority over football. That his chances of making it to the NFL are slim to none.

"What is your plan?" I ask, wanting to get this conversation over with.

Noah stares at me for a beat. "I asked Ethan to become your accountability partner. He's willing to meet up with you to help you figure out—"

"Absolutely not," I say immediately, my hackles rising. "I don't need an accountability partner. I just need a little more time to turn my grades around."

Noah crosses his arms over his chest. "Whatever you're doing isn't working."

My lips close. Goddamn him. I want to say something cutting, but I can't when I know his bossiness is only coming from a place of fear. He's asked me multiple times over the last several months if I'm doing okay. I've withdrawn from him since everything went down with Mason. I used to visit his apartment regularly, but I can't do it now. I'll be damned if I let Mason see how much his presence affects me.

And if I'm truly honest with myself, I'm afraid of him.

I haven't been able to reason away the buzzing that starts in my head—the heart palpitations and clammy hands—the handful of times I've seen him since everything happened.

None of it is Noah's fault. If he knew what Mason did, he'd move out of that apartment in a heartbeat. Hell, he'd probably even push me to go to the cops, which I'd never do.

Even knowing all that doesn't make me resent Noah any less. Somehow, his close proximity to Mason feels like a betrayal. It's irrational, but I can't make the feeling go away. Just like how I can't stop myself from ruminating on the events of that night and wishing I made different choices.

I narrow my eyes on Noah's face. "It was an invasion of my privacy to bring Ethan into this. He already told me he knows all about my academic struggles. You had no right to say anything."

Noah opens his mouth to speak, but Ethan talks over him. "She's right." His tone is firm. "You should have asked her permission before you brought me into this."

Noah's eyes grow huge, and I can't stop my jaw from falling open. I place my hands on my hips as I turn to Ethan. "What the hell is this? You're on *my* side?"

Ethan stands up straighter. "On this subject at least. He shouldn't have asked me to be your accountability partner without getting you on board first. Still..." He squares his broad shoulders. "I agree with him that you need help. Whatever you're doing now *isn't* working."

Anger flames in my chest, and I raise my chin. "I can't focus at all lately. I don't see how you're going to fix that. Do you plan to do my goddamn work for me?"

I expected to annoy him, but his expression has grown...soft somehow. He tilts his head as he studies me. "Why can't you focus? What's changed recently?"

My heart jumps into my throat. Somehow it feels like he can see inside my mind. That he knows what happened with Mason.

That's crazy. Mason wouldn't have told a soul what happened.

He denied that anything happened at all. And he threatened that if I ever shared what *didn't* happen, he'd send his family lawyer after me for defamation.

The chances of him succeeding with a claim like that are remote. I've done my research. Still, it would bring scrutiny onto me that I'm not ready to deal with.

I just want to forget everything, to go back to the girl I used to be.

"It doesn't matter why you can't focus," Noah says. "Because Ethan's going to help you do exactly that. Each week, you'll meet up and figure out a game plan. The next week, you'll review what worked and what didn't." He smiles. "He'll be just like a coach."

I roll my eyes. "You mean he'll be my parole officer."

"I won't be your parole officer," Ethan cuts in. "I'll let you set the pace. You tell me how you want things to go, and I'll listen."

I snort. "Listening isn't one of your finer qualities, Ethan."

Ethan's eyes fill with an emotion I can't quite pinpoint. Is he hurt that I think he's a bad listener? Strange. I've said much meaner things to him in the past. Hell, two nights ago I called him a joy vacuum, and he laughed.

"I want you to start logging your activities," Noah says. "It's a great time-management hack. You can see how you spend your time and decide if there are better ways to utilize it."

I release an unsteady breath. "Who gets to decide the best way to utilize my time, Ethan or me?"

"You," Ethan answers right away. "You're the ultimate judge. I'll just be there to help you brainstorm. You're in charge, Lily. I know you think I boss you around, that I'm not good at listening... I won't be like that. I promise."

"Brace yourself," I say. "I don't think it will be easy for you."

Ethan's eyes twinkle. "I've survived your viciousness for over two years now. After that, I can handle anything."

My breath catches slightly, and my heart gives an unexpected flutter. When did Ethan start matching my energy and teasing me back? I shouldn't be warmed by it. He's probably just trying to manipulate me. To get me to agree to this stupid plan for Noah's sake.

"We both have your best interests at heart," Noah says. "You might feel like I'm being a dick with all this, but I'm doing it because I'm worried about you."

My cheeks suffuse with heat. Worried. I hate that word so much. It's so fucking condescending. I don't want anyone's useless worry. What I want is to fix my stupid sleep and grades and forget about Mason forever.

I ought to tell both Noah and Ethan to go to hell, but is that what the old Lily would do? I don't think so. She'd probably go along with this plan and use it as an opportunity to antagonize Ethan, her favorite thing to do.

A pleasant thrill runs down my spine. It could be fun to meet up with Ethan every week and tease him incessantly.

I shoot Ethan a lazy smile. "When do we start?"

Ethan's eyes flicker with confusion and then settle on my mouth. Shit, this is weird. It's the same look he gave me right before that kiss.

"You'll need to give it a few days," Noah says, and the hungry look on Ethan's face vanishes in a flash.

"Lily needs to start collecting data on her daily habits." Noah's expression grows stern. "Make a spreadsheet and write down every single thing you do in a day and how much time it takes. I do mean every single activity. Believe me, it works. Even just collecting the data will make you more productive."

I groan. "Oh my God, that sounds like torture."

"If that sounds like torture, you must not be doing any work at all." Noah's tone is biting. "It's not that hard to log your activities. It takes seconds."

He only says that because he doesn't have ADHD. He wasn't cursed with the inability to focus on anything that isn't remotely interesting.

My biggest problem is that hardly anything interests me at all anymore, outside of the few hours a week I have alone with my paints, canvases, and brushes.

"Noah, she doesn't need this right now," Ethan says. "Lily, if logging your activities doesn't work, we'll nix it. It's just a strategy to try. Like I said before, you're in charge. I'll work with you."

A comforting glow spreads through me. I ought to find his coddling condescending, but it's so difficult when he's staring at me with such a warm expression. Ethan is usually all hard edges and firm commands.

"How about we meet in three days?" Ethan says. "You can come next door when I'm done with practice. Six o'clock."

I smile mischievously. "I'll be there."

And I'm going to make Ethan wish he never agreed to this.

Chapter Five

E than

My tennis shoes pound against the pavement. I'm probably killing my knees, and my posture is atrocious. If Coach Rodriguez saw me now, he'd be appalled. This was supposed to be my endurance run, so why am I furiously sprinting?

It's almost like I'm trying to work thoughts of Lily out of my body.

I have my first appointment with her tonight, and I've thought about nothing else these last three days. I've barely been able to focus on football, school, or church.

This is insanity.

Where are you, God? I've asked you again and again to take away this strange new obsession with Lily.

I've never felt God, and that's the problem. Something must be broken inside me. I'm more disciplined in my faith than even Brandon, and he's a pastor. I read my Bible every night and never miss church. I always volunteer for community outreach projects, even when my schedule is nearly maxed out with football and school.

And yet God never speaks to me. I talk to him all the time, but I never hear his voice, never see signs in the world—no shivers down my spine or bursts of sunlight breaking through the clouds.

The most heavenly experience I've ever had was kissing a girl with stormy-gray eyes and plump pink mouth.

"Hey, Ethan!" A voice slices through my blasphemous thoughts.

When I look over my shoulder, Kinsley is behind me, sprinting in my direction. I slow my pace to a jog.

"Mind if I run with you for a bit?" she asks as she catches up to me. "You'll have to slow way down, Number Forty-Four."

I force a smile. "Sure."

The truth is I'd much rather be alone. Kinsley might be my church friend, but she's much closer to Lily. I can't look at her without thinking of Lily.

As if I even need a reminder when she hasn't left my damn head in three days.

Kinsley and I fall into a rhythm side by side. "Bible study was interesting last week," Kinsley says after a while.

I frown. "You mean Emma and Dylan's engagement?"

She hums in agreement. "Emma is nineteen. She still lives with her parents. It's insane to me that they both think they're old enough to get married. My biggest struggle with being a Christian in college is that I didn't come here to get my MRS degree. I don't relate to people who did."

"You're not alone. I have no plans to get married any time soon."

"Really? That kind of surprises me because—" She pauses. "Shit. I was about to say something really inappropriate. Ignore me."

I turn to her and smile. "You were about to say you're surprised because I'm planning to stay a virgin until marriage. It's okay. I know it's weird. Even my brother thinks I'm too traditional."

She grins. "I still can't believe Brandon—the hot pastor of Santa Barbara—is your brother. It's like having two celebrities in one family."

I chuckle, trying to hide my discomfort. Somehow, even after over three years of being on the Hawks, I'm still not accustomed to the spotlight and attention that comes with it. It's especially unsettling that now—after the scouts started attending our games—I'm even more widely known than Brandon.

Seeing myself on a TV screen for the first time was surreal, and not in a good way. I can't relax knowing that any mistake I make is under the examination of people who don't even know me. I strive to never make mistakes in the first place, but no one is perfect. I'd hate to let down people who look up to me, and now that I have national attention, that pool of people has grown significantly.

"So I wanted to talk to you..." Kinsley says.

Something about the hesitance in her voice makes my skin grow prickly. Is it possible that she witnessed my kiss with Lily? That light did go on in Lily's bedroom shortly afterward. It could have been Kinsley, and she would have had a perfect view of us.

"Okay..." I murmur.

"This might seem like an awkward question, but are you close with Mason?"

"No," I say immediately, relief coursing through my veins. "He's not one of my favorite people."

When I glance her way, she's nodding slowly. "Good, because I have to ask you an uncomfortable question. I'm overstepping by even talking to you. Lily told me nothing about why they broke up, and she'd be pissed if she knew that I went to you for information, but I don't know what else to do. Lily barely talks to me anymore, and she's been different since they broke up. I wonder if he did something to her..." She shuts her eyes for a moment as she shakes her head. "My suspicions are probably crazy. I don't know if I should even voice them."

The hairs on my arms stand up. I halt my step and turn to Kinsley, who also comes to a stop. When I search her face, my anxiety only grows. She looks deeply troubled.

What the hell does she mean that Mason may have done something to Lily? Is she implying he hurt Lily?

I'll fucking kill him if he did.

"Don't beat around the bush," I say sharply. "You're not going to hurt my feelings talking shit about Mason."

"No." Kinsley takes a few steps back. "I really shouldn't be talking to you about this. I think Lily would be hurt, and I'm probably being paranoid. I'm sorry if I worried you. It's all probably fine."

With that, she turns around and starts jogging away.

I stand there for who knows how long, my head spinning. What was Kinsley getting at?

The back of my neck prickles, and an otherworldly aura settles over me. My gaze roams up over the palm tree next to me, and something about it looks hazy and dreamlike.

Holy fuck. I think this might be a sign from God.

My first ever.

Maybe he wants me to help Lily because her struggles in school have something to do with Mason. That asshole hurt her in some way, just like Noah suspected he might.

If it was physical, I really will kill him.

No, that's crazy. Kinsley probably just meant he messed with Lily emotionally, though...that seems strange. Mason isn't the sharpest tool in the shed. I think Lily could run circles around him with her sass.

Still, if she really liked him, it would have made her vulnerable to getting hurt. Hell, maybe she even loved him. An unpleasant feeling twists in my gut, but I try to ignore it. It's not jealousy. My brain is just mixed up after that kiss.

How can I possibly help her? She can't stand me. She

certainly wouldn't want to tell me her troubles if she's not even willing to share them with Kinsley.

Still, I can't reason away this strange sensation. It's like an invisible hand guiding me, urging me forward despite my doubts.

I asked for God to speak to me, and he has.

Maybe I can help Lily by just being there, showing her that I'm steady and loyal. I can help her work on her studies with the utmost patience. I won't be the uptight version of myself who she thinks is a prick. I'll open my heart and try to be a real friend.

If I can earn her trust, maybe she will open up to me about why she's been so troubled and unable to focus lately.

Exhilaration pumps through my veins. My recent obsession with her might not be sinful at all. Maybe it was God's way of showing me that I'm exactly where I'm supposed to be. Maybe I'm being called by him to help her.

If that's the case, I can never, *ever* touch her again.

Chapter Six

L ily

My stomach flutters as I knock on the door of the frat house. The prospect of teasing Ethan for a full hour fills me with a strange sense of purpose, something I haven't felt in months. I ought to be embarrassed that such childish behavior can make me feel like my old self, but I'll take these small wins as they come.

Ethan is all business in his approach to everything. He'll be aggravated out of his mind if he feels like I'm not taking this whole "accountability partner" thing seriously.

It will be his own fault. He overstepped by agreeing to this. Even he admitted that.

The door opens, revealing Ethan's tall form. The warmth in his eyes makes my smile fade. Why does he look so excited to see me?

His demeanor toward me has changed since that night. I wasn't imagining it during the meeting with Noah. He's some-how...softer, more inviting.

I brush off the thought as I walk inside and follow him down the hallway. I won't let his new warmth stop me from teasing him. I'll make it my mission to bring out that grumpy, exasperated Ethan who never fails to amuse me.

He leads me inside a room that looks like a library.

"What is this?" I ask, my gaze drifting over the wall-to-ceiling bookshelves.

"We call it the study."

I snort. "Pretentious."

"Yes. Especially coming from a group of guys who hold a monthly beer chugging competition. No one uses our study except me." He pauses for a beat. "Because I'm pretentious, I guess."

When I whip my head in his direction, he's smiling faintly—a sweet little quirk of the lips—but it's nearly blinding. My God, this man is beautiful when he smiles. It sure beats his usual stoic frown. I was never affected by his looks until recently, but then again, I don't think he's ever smiled at me like that before.

I turn away, pretending to examine a shelf of books. "I wouldn't say pretentious. That's not your brand of asshole. Don't be offended by my use of the word 'asshole.' We all have our own unique brand, even me."

"Oh, yeah? What's my brand?"

I frown at the question. It's not like him to indulge my rambling silliness. "I'd call you the intellectual gym rat. You're analytical about your approach to athletic and academic excellence, and it makes you feel like you're better than people who don't work as hard as you do. It's totally insufferable, but it doesn't matter because you're hot. You don't need a personality when you have nothing to compensate for."

When he bursts into laughter, heat breaks out over my cheeks. I just told him he doesn't have a personality, damn it. I've said versions of the same thing many times, and he almost always rolls his eyes.

"I love how you hide your viciousness in backhanded compliments," he says, his voice strained from laughter. "You tried to disarm me by saying I'm hot, and then you followed it up by basically calling me a dumb jock. Your sass is almost Machiavellian, Lily."

The warmth in his voice sends a pleasant tingle over my skin. When I turn around, his eyes are soft and affectionate.

Who the fuck is this playful version of Ethan?

I swallow. "I only have a vague idea of what Machiavellian means. I was a C student before my grades started failing. Maybe this is our cue to start our...accountability session, or whatever."

"In a minute." He takes a step in my direction. "You haven't told me what your brand of asshole is. I'm dying of curiosity."

My head grows fuzzy. This isn't going according to plan. He's supposed to be annoyed that I'm distracting him from our session with my teasing, not asking me for more.

"My brand of asshole is the most insufferable of all," I say, "but I take care not to let it show."

"Insufferable how?"

"I'm vain. I think I'm the most delightful person in the world. The most fun. The life of the party. Not the prettiest girl at the party, mind you, but always the drunkest."

Ethan snorts, shaking his head. He believes this to be true, no doubt, and I almost believe it myself. I'm performing for him right now. Pretending to be the girl I once was.

Is that what my plan to tease him was all about, really? I wanted to annoy Ethan so I could feel like my old self, if only for an hour.

How sad.

"If there's a pole," I say, striving for lightness. "I will be dancing on it. If there's a karaoke machine, you bet your ass I'll be belting out 'Wildest Dreams' at the top of my lungs. Off-key, of course. Fun people don't need to be good at anything. We'll always get jobs because we're personality hires. I'm extremely smug about this. I pity people who don't know how to have fun."

"Like me," he says without flinching, and my smile fades.

No, Ethan. I pity myself. I'm not that wild, boisterous girl I used to be, and I'm not sure if I ever will be again.

"You're wrong about one thing," he says. "You're always one of the prettiest girls at the party."

I shake my head sharply, even as my stomach flutters. He's called me pretty before, but he was only being polite. Ethan is, above all, a gentleman. He'd never let a girl call herself unattractive without contradicting her.

"My personality confuses people," I say. "I'm so much fun that it distracts from the flaws in my face."

"What flaws?"

I wave a hand. "Stop with the flattery. You think I'm being humble, and it couldn't be further from the truth. I'm saying my personality is so spectacular that no one notices my average looks. Do you know what a gift that is? I could rule the world someday."

He stares at me with such warmth, I could almost call it tenderness. My stomach flips over. The little speech I gave was so vain it bordered on obnoxious. I never would have said it to anyone but Ethan. Someone who already thinks I'm a frivolous party girl without a deep thought in her head.

Nothing about this meeting is going the way I planned.

"How about we get to our session?" I say. "I'm excited to show you my activity log. I was very meticulous."

And I included an item that's going to make his eyes pop out of his head. When he scolds me for it, I'll remind him that Noah told me to log every single activity.

Ethan frowns, but he gestures for me to sit down at a big wooden desk in the corner of the room.

My head starts to swim. Maybe I shouldn't have rushed this part of our meeting. I don't want to talk about my grades for the better part of an hour. I want to shut them out of my mind and pretend they don't matter.

"Are you okay?" Ethan asks, snapping me into the present. He's now sitting in front of the desk. When did he move?

Damn, I was zoning out. This twilight hour is always difficult for me. My brain is ready to shut down. The problem is it never does. Once I enter my bedroom, my adrenaline spikes, and my thoughts start racing. No amount of exhaustion can bring me down.

"I've been having trouble sleeping lately," I find myself admitting. "Probably because I'm stressed about my grades."

He tilts his head. "How long has this been going on?"

"Months." I plop down on the seat opposite Ethan.

"Lily, that's not good."

The concern in his voice draws my gaze to his face. He's staring at me with a furrowed brow. "Sleep is essential to productivity. No wonder you've been having trouble focusing."

I shrug. "There's not much I can do about it."

"That's not true. You need to see a doctor. Nothing I suggest will help you if you're not sleeping."

"I already went to a doctor. He gave me Ambien, which didn't work."

Ethan frowns. "Then you should try something else. When we're done here, I'll write you a whole list of supplements you can try."

I give him a thumbs up. "Sounds good, Coach."

He nods. "Let's get to your log. We'll talk about sleep more when we wrap up, but there's something I want to mention before we get started. It might be awkward, but it needs to be said. We're going to be spending quite a bit of time together over these next few weeks, and given recent events..." His lips purse. "You don't have to worry about me kissing you again. It'll never happen."

I grit my teeth. Of course golden boy Ethan would take Noah's misogynistic rule about no teammates touching his sister as seriously as the word of God. He already told me that he's never going to kiss me again. Does he think I've been on pins and needles waiting for another kiss?

"Damn." I huff. "I was hoping for constant kisses. I never

study without kissing. The two things go together like peanut butter and jelly. How will I get through the next hour?"

Ethan tries to smile, but the movement is tight. His cheeks flush, and his eyes dart to my mouth, lingering there. Heat pools in my belly.

Is he really getting flustered at the mere mention of kissing me?

Interesting.

"Well." He clears his throat, shifting in his seat. "I guess we'll have to find some other way to keep you focused. Can I see your daily log?"

"Sure." I'm grateful that he changed the subject. I'd rather not think about kissing him again either.

It was a delicious kiss—sweet and sensual. The perfect antidote to my recent revulsion of being touched by any man.

I pull out my laptop and flip it open. The excel spreadsheet is still up on the screen. "I've accounted for every single minute of my day." I slide my open laptop across the desk. "It was so mind-numbingly boring, I wanted to claw my eyes out."

Boring isn't the right word, though. The effort it took to document my day was nothing short of herculean. Attention to detail makes me want to bash my head against a wall, especially lately when focus is so difficult to harness.

Ethan's gaze drifts over the screen. "Like I said, if it doesn't work, we'll try something else. This is supposed to—" His lips close, and his eyes grow huge.

I strain my throat to keep from laughing. I know exactly what he just saw.

The single entry I wrote just for Ethan. It wasn't even true, but I had to include it. It's something the old Lily would have done. She'd have followed Noah's law to the letter just to disconcert Ethan.

11:30 a.m. Watched porn and masturbated

"Lily." Ethan's voice is probing.

"What?"

"You don't need to write down every single thing you do."

"But Noah said—"

"Don't give me that. You know why you wrote this down."

The huskiness in his tone startles me. When I lift my gaze, his face is flushed. Oh wow. I really flustered him.

"Alright, fine," I say. "I wanted to embarrass you."

To my surprise, a faint smile tugs at his lips. "I'm not embarrassed. It's a normal thing to do."

A sudden jolt tingles through my body, and my mouth falls open. "Are you saying you watch porn and masturbate too?"

His face grows utterly still, and his throat works. "I try not to watch porn, because I've read that the industry is corrupt. But I do masturbate."

I slap my hand over my mouth. "Oh my God, Ethan. You have no idea how happy this makes me. I really thought you were so religious and uptight you wouldn't even masturbate. So if you don't look at porn, what do you think about when you do it? I need porn because I'm a visual girlie. I like thrusting bodies and moans."

He stares at me for a long moment, as if in indecision. Shit. I think his face is growing damp.

What a liar. He *is* embarrassed.

Still, I never thought he'd share something like this openly with me. The thought of Ethan with his hands moving up and down his cock with his face as flushed as it is now...

Fuck. I almost wish I hadn't left that entry.

In a flash, the discomfort on his face vanishes. "You truly are Machiavellian. You know what you're doing right now."

"I told you I don't even know what that word means." I frown. "So no, I don't know what I'm doing."

He shakes his head. "It means you're smart and strategic against your enemies, and you use their weaknesses to your advantage. You didn't give me those graphic details because you have no filter. You did it because you know I don't want to imagine you..."

His eyes widen minutely, and he scratches the back of his head. A charged silence follows, and the air grows thick as mud.

Holy shit. Was Ethan about to admit that he pictured *me* masturbating? The thought makes a delicious pressure build in my tummy.

I school my expression to look innocent. "Doesn't want to imagine me what?"

He lifts a hand. "Stop. This conversation is over."

"But you're my coach. You need to spell things out for me when I don't understand."

He groans. "You're the fucking worst, Lily Greenwood."

Warmth rushes through my veins. My God, I haven't had this much fun in months. How bizarre that it would be in the company of stick-up-his-ass Ethan Harrington.

Maybe I've misjudged him. At least a little.

A while later, Ethan looks up from my laptop. "I have to say, I'm impressed with your attention to detail. You logged every day to the minute."

His tone is gentle but ever so slightly condescending. I grit my teeth. "You don't need to praise me for something a ten-year-old could have done."

"Did it help?"

I let out a long sigh. "If I'm being honest, it was distracting. I'm having such a hard time focusing in general. It sucked having another thing to do. It took my attention away from things that actually matter."

"Then we don't need to do it anymore. The whole point is to find strategies that work for you."

"I don't think anything's going to work." I rub my temples to ease the tightness in my scalp. "I can't think straight. My brain hasn't worked since I stopped sleeping."

"How much sleep are you getting?"

"Like four hours a night, if I'm lucky."

"Four hours a night?" He sounds appalled. "That's insane. How long has this been going on?"

A shiver runs down my spine. There's something in his voice... Something probing, like he knows that my lack of sleep was caused by a single event.

That's crazy. I'm reading signs that aren't there.

There's no way he could possibly know that I could tell him the exact date when I stopped sleeping. April fourth. The night after...everything happened.

Crazy. Mason overpowered my body for ten minutes, and I'm still facing the repercussions six months later.

I know what he did was a terrible thing, but I didn't think I was this type of woman. How could I have let my life spiral out of control because of a man?

"It's been months." I keep my answer vague, not wanting Ethan's meticulous brain to trace my problems back to my relationship with Mason.

"No wonder your grades are suffering. Do you know how important sleep is for your brain? You literally can't function without it."

"What do you expect me to do about it? Telling myself I need to sleep won't make it happen."

"No, but we can try strategies to get you to sleep. We'll come up with a plan."

I snort. "Good luck with that."

"Here's what we're going to do." He snaps my laptop shut. "I don't care about Noah's plans for our meetings. We're nixing them. I don't want you to even think about schoolwork before bed. It's only going to stress you out and make it harder to sleep. We'll take a walk." He twists around to look out the window. "The sun is setting now, and I've read sunsets get our brains ready for sleep—something about the light. We'll head over to a campus coffee shop and get you some chamomile tea."

"Ethan, you're making sleep sound like homework."

"You got a better idea, Greenwood?"

His sternness makes a smile rise to my lips. In Ethan's mind, every problem has a solution if you just follow the right steps. He's so confident that he's nearly convincing me that he can help me sleep tonight when nothing has worked so far. Then again, I haven't tried much of anything besides my late-night walks.

"I don't have a better idea," I say. "Let's do this, Coach."

He grins. "I like the sound of that. From now on, I'm your sleep coach." He stands up from the desk and crosses his arms over his chest, looking as commanding as his own Coach Rodriguez. "On your feet. Now. And no more whining."

As I stand, warmth spreads through me. I ought to be annoyed that he accused me of whining, instead I find his high-handedness strangely...cute. It must be months of sleep deprivation making me delirious.

Chapter Seven

E than

The coffee shop is much emptier than usual, probably because we arrived an hour before closing. As we sit across from each other, Lily takes a sip of her chamomile tea and grimaces. Her nose scrunches up, looking so cute I want to kiss it.

Fuck this. I thought I'd gotten my recent attraction to her under control, at least for our hour together. When our session began, my focus was on helping her relax and warm up to me so she could potentially open up about Mason. It seemed to be working. We were getting along better than we ever have.

It all went to hell when I saw that entry in her spreadsheet. A vivid image immediately appeared in my head. Her head thrown back with her pretty lips parted and those big eyes glazed. Her little hand working frantically between her thighs. *"Oh God, Ethan,"* she whispered.

And then when she started getting specific, saying she needs a visual...

What if I gave her that visual?

My cock grew so uncomfortably hard, I had to discreetly adjust myself, praying that she wouldn't notice.

I've had a handful of sexual thoughts about her over the years. Maybe her kneeling in front of me or naked on my bed. They stopped there. I forced my brain to go somewhere else while I beat my cock.

I didn't want to want her. I tried to convince myself I didn't, that it was only a passing thought that came from nowhere.

What if it wasn't? What if this recent attraction was actually lying dormant all along?

"Can I at least put honey in this horrendous tea?" Lily asks, thankfully pulling me from my head.

"No. Honey is basically sugar. You don't want to spike your insulin before bed."

Her eyelids flutter. "I've eaten candy before bed and slept fine. I can promise you my lack of sleep has nothing to do with sugar."

"You don't know that for sure. This is just something we're trying. A sleep ritual. Chamomile tea and relaxing conversation."

She sucks in her lips to fight a smile.

"What?"

"Ethan, nothing about you is relaxing."

"How about I start talking about myself? That should put you right to sleep."

"Great idea." Her face lights up as she sits up straighter. "I have a question for you."

A smile rises to my lips. I love that she didn't contradict me when I basically called myself boring. There's something so playful about her teasing. I can't explain it, but it makes me feel accepted. Flaws and all.

"What?" I ask.

"Why do you live the life of a fifty-five-year-old man with acid reflux? Noah tells me you don't even eat after a certain time every night, and you take a million supplements every day. I don't understand it. If I looked like you—" she gestures at my chest "—I'd eat In-N-Out five times a day."

My gut clenches, like it does every time she even hints that I'm attractive. Crazy. I've gotten enough validation over the years to know I'm a good-looking guy.

And it doesn't matter to Lily that I'm good-looking. She's speaking about me now like I'm a biological specimen under her examination. Hell, she just compared me to a fifty-five-year-old man with acid reflux.

"What's the point of working out so much if you can't enjoy the benefits?" she asks.

I shrug. "I want to be the best version of myself, especially when I have this chance of making it to the NFL. I can't control everything that happens on the field. There are too many moving pieces. Keeping my brain and body in top shape is one of the few things I can control."

She rubs her thumb along the cardboard sleeve of her cup. "It doesn't sound fun. In fact, it sounds kind of miserable."

A chill skitters over my skin. My frat brothers and teammates constantly tease me about being a control freak, but holy shit, no one has called me miserable before. How many people can say that NFL scouts are attending their games just to see them? I'm one of the luckiest people I know.

She must sense my unease, because her face softens. "I mean... I'm sure you're not miserable, but it just seems that way to me. It's probably because we're built differently. I like parties and movie nights and painting, and you like...working out and taking supplements."

When I snort out a laugh, she smiles sheepishly. "I'm sure you have a lot of other hobbies. I don't know you that well."

I scratch the back of my head. "I don't do much else besides football, school, and church stuff, but that won't always be the case. I'm good at delaying gratification. I can put in the work now for a later reward."

"Damn," she mutters. "I wish I had your discipline. It's not fair. Have you always been this way?"

"Pretty much. I had a high GPA in high school, even though I was constantly busy with football and church. I don't know, Lily." I smile. "Maybe it's all part of my brand of asshole. I don't have a personality, right? It frees up a lot of time in my schedule."

She scoffs. "You do have a personality. You know I was just being a dick when I said you don't. My guess is you have high-achieving parents. I'll bet they're both top CEOs or something. That would explain why you live in the fanciest frat house in the whole Greek scene."

"No," I say immediately. "Nothing could be further from the truth. My brother pays for my tuition and rent, though I plan to pay him back someday. My dad left when I was eight, thankfully, but my mom has always struggled to make ends meet. That's why I'm so on top of my grades and football performance. If I don't make it to the NFL, I at least need a really good job. I want to take care of her, to make up for the fact that she had to work so hard to support me."

Her eyes are wide and unfocused. "You said 'thankfully.'"

I frown. "What do you mean?"

"You said 'thankfully' your dad left. That's kind of a weird thing to say."

My jaw tightens as I try to keep my voice steady. "Yeah, my dad is a giant prick. To both me and my mom. Everything had to be in perfect order. My mom had to keep the house spotless. I wasn't allowed to step out of line in any way or else he'd lose it on me. As if he had the moral high ground." Anger flares in my gut. "He expected perfection from us, and then he left. For another woman."

"Ah." Lily nods slowly. "That must be where your whole virgin thing comes from."

The tension leaves my shoulders as I chuckle. I can never predict where her brain is going to go, which makes conversations with her a wild ride. I'm never bored.

"My virgin thing?" I say. "I've never heard it called that before. You mean my plan to save myself for marriage?"

"Yeah."

I frown. "Why do you think that would have something to do with my dad?"

Lily's brows draw together. "If I had a dad who wanted me to be all perfect and moral, and then he cheated on my mom... I'd probably be like, 'Fuck you. I'll be a virgin 'til I'm married just to show you I'm better than you.'"

Warmth fills my chest, and I want to kiss her yet again. I love the way she sees the world. It's so Lily-centered, and yet it doesn't feel selfish. It's like she's speaking from a place of unfiltered truth. She doesn't give a shit if she appears selfish, and that makes her raw honesty comforting.

The truth is I do sometimes revel in my moral superiority over my dad. It's a feeling I try to stifle, because it's petty and prideful, but hearing it from Lily's mouth makes me feel...less alone.

"That's not why I'm a virgin," I say. "Or at least, I don't think it is, because I'm not a psychologist."

She frowns. "Why are you a virgin? It's so weird."

"I love how blunt you are. I know it's weird. I actually don't think having sex outside of marriage is wrong for everyone. My brother is a pretty liberal pastor, and he helped me see that, but I know it's wrong for me."

She grimaces. "I don't even want to get married. If I were you, I'd be committing to no sex at all."

"Oh, yeah?" I say, trying to keep my voice light even as my chest fills with an uncomfortable heaviness.

This feeling isn't rational. Why should I care that Lily doesn't want to get married? It's not like I'd ever want to marry her.

"Yep." Lily flips her hair over her shoulder. "Men in our society think they own you if you're married. Fuck that. I value my freedom more than anything."

I swallow. "What if you found a guy who didn't treat you like he owned you? A guy you trusted to respect your freedom?"

"Then he'd respect my wishes not to get married." She narrows her eyes on my face. "And what about you? What if you fall in love with a woman who doesn't want to get married?"

I shake my head sharply. "She wouldn't be the woman for me. I know I want to get married. I know I want to stay a virgin until I do. It was a vow I made to myself and my future wife years ago, and I take vows seriously."

Her eyebrows lift, and her mouth parts. She looks so appalled that I can't wait to hear what she's going to say next.

"Ethan." Her voice is full of disbelief. "You don't even know your future wife. She's basically imaginary. And the only other person you made this vow to was yourself. Let me tell you something about a promise to yourself—" she raises both hands in the air "—no one's going to punish you for breaking it."

I smile, my body feeling as light as it has in months. "You bring up some excellent points, but you have to understand that I'm a Christian. We see the world differently."

"I mean, I get it, but you didn't even mention God when you talked about your virginity. Apparently, this vow was only to yourself and your future wife."

Shock vibrates through my body, making my head grow fuzzy. Holy shit, she's right. I somehow had an entire conversation about staying pure until marriage without even mentioning my relationship with God.

Because he feels so distant, like a memory that fades every time I reach for it.

Before I can respond, Lily's eyes dart to a table in the corner of the coffee shop. Her lips curl into a mischievous smile. She sets her elbows on the wooden table and leans forward. "My crush is here," she whispers.

Crush? What crush?

I whip my head in the direction of the table and spot a single guy in a group of girls. That must be him. He's tall and lanky with light-blond hair. Relatively good-looking, I guess.

I dislike him on sight.

"Oh my God, Ethan," Lily mutters. "You're as obvious as a fire alarm."

When my gaze flickers back to her, she's glaring at me.

I sigh. "I'm sorry. I shouldn't have looked at...your crush."

"It's alright." Her expression grows cheeky. "You don't know any better. You're a tall, handsome man. The world gave you a free pass on developing social graces."

I snort. "This again. I thought you said I do have a personality—"

My lips close when the guy starts walking in our direction. Lily's attention is fully on him now, her eyes sparkling. I clench my jaw, and a prickling heat spreads across my skin.

"Hey, Jake," Lily says.

Jake. What a basic bro name.

Lily and Jake exchange polite conversation, something about a class they share, but I hardly hear them. My attention is fixed on the way Jake's gaze lingers on Lily's mouth.

My fists clench under the table. That pretty mouth of hers feels like it's mine after kissing her.

What the hell is wrong with me? Lily has been with countless guys in the time since Noah introduced me to her over two years ago. I've never really liked it, but I never felt possessive of her.

I'm pulled out of my daze when Lily gestures at me. "This is Ethan, my brother's best friend. He's my new tutor. Don't be shocked, Jake. I know you were probably thinking I'm a stellar student after all the times you've seen me sneak into class a half hour late."

Jake grins at Lily like he's delighted with her, and it takes all my willpower to keep from scowling at him.

I know Lily gave that overly wordy explanation about who I am for a reason. She wants to make it very clear to Jake that I'm not her boyfriend.

"It's getting late," I blurt out. "We should go soon."

Lily looks startled as she glances at me, and I want to wince. I'm acting like a dick.

"Um..." Jake scratches the back of his head, looking nervous. He examines my face for a moment before turning to Lily. "Can I get your number? I feel like we hang out with a lot of the same people, but we've never connected for some reason."

I want to scoff. What a spineless way to ask for a woman's number, couching it in excuses. If I had a crush on Lily, I'd set a date with her for the very next day. Tell her outright that she's the only woman I think about.

If I had a crush on her.

Lily's face lights up as Jake hands her his phone. A sour taste rises in my throat. A moment later, Jake is gone, but I don't feel any better.

"Ready to go, Grumplestiltskin?" Lily cocks a brow at me, her expression so accusing I want to wince.

"I guess I was rude to interrupt you guys." I stand up from my chair. "I just wanted to get you home soon." I shoot her a mock stern look. "You need to get to bed by nine o'clock, Greenwood. You'll be getting a text from your coach in the morning to see if our sleep routine worked."

She rolls her eyes as she grabs her bag from the floor. "What other fun activities do you have lined up for me?"

Her sass eases the tension in my shoulders. "Don't use that tone with your coach, or I'll make you do push-ups until you beg for mercy."

She snorts. "I'll be begging for mercy after one."

A warm smile rises to my lips as we walk out of the coffee shop. I love how she embraces her flaws without a second thought.

"I want you to keep track of everything you do before bed and how much you sleep," I say. "Be expecting daily texts from me over the next week."

"Got it."

An unexpected thrill runs down my spine. I ought to be

alarmed that the prospect of texting her every day exhilarates me, but maybe it's yet another sign that I'm exactly where God wants me.

I was called to help Lily, and damn it, I'm going to do it. If being close to her messes with my head, so be it. My will is stronger than my desires. I'm not in danger of kissing her again.

Chapter Eight

L ily

The early morning light is soft, casting a gentle glow over the porch of my sorority house. I'm sitting cross-legged on an old wooden chair with a canvas propped up on an easel in front of me. As I move my brush, colors blend across the canvas. It's quiet outside, except for the occasional chirping of birds and the faint rustle of leaves in the breeze.

It's sometime after six a.m., and I slept five hours last night. An improvement. I forced myself to follow Ethan's sleep ritual to the letter. He told me on our walk home last night that if I had to get up during the night, only relaxing activities were allowed. So when my brain wouldn't stop buzzing around midnight, I came out here and set up this easel.

His advice worked. After about a half hour of painting in near darkness, I found myself nodding off. Without even cleaning my paints and palate in the sink, I wandered back into my room, plopped down on my bed, and drifted into oblivion for a few more hours.

It was heaven for a short while.

The porch door creaks, and footsteps thump on the patio. A moment later, Kinsley appears at my side. She's still in her pj's with a coffee cup in hand.

"Look at you," she says, her voice raspy. "Painting at sunrise. What a romantic way to spend your morning."

I dip my brush in a powder-blue paint. "It's only because I'm an insomniac."

Kinsley sighs. "Still?"

"Yep. Nothing works. I've even tried Ambien." A smile rises to my lips. "Ethan made me drink chamomile tea last night, which was disgusting."

"Ethan?" Kinsley's voice is full of curiosity.

So I tell her the story of how Noah assigned Ethan to be my accountability partner. I even tell her about how Ethan has recently become my sleep coach.

Her eyes widen. "Sleep coach?"

"You know how Ethan is. So disciplined about everything. He's turning my sleep into homework. Literally. He texted me a whole list of things to try each night, and he's going to check in with me every morning to see how I slept."

Kinsley cocks a brow. "I can think of a great way he can help you sleep. Too bad he's saving himself for marriage."

"We had a whole conversation about that yesterday. He told me he doesn't think having sex outside of marriage is wrong, but it's wrong for him. How bizarre."

She nods slowly. "He's talked about that in our church college group. Honestly..." She pauses for a moment. "He doesn't seem like he cares that much about it—staying a virgin, I mean. It almost feels like... He's trying to prove how disciplined he is."

I snort. "As if he needs any more proof. That man is as uptight as a drill sergeant."

"So true. No one needs to get laid more than he does. I've

never believed in the whole purity culture bullshit. Jesus doesn't care about our sex lives."

"I don't even know what purity culture is, but it sounds—"

My phone buzzes on the small table beside me. My heart flutters when Ethan's name appears. I reach down and unlock the screen.

Ethan: How many hours?

I shut my eyes as I smile. What an Ethan question. He needs to know the exact number of hours I slept. He might even be logging it on a spreadsheet for me. He's so meticulous.

I type back quickly.

Me: Five hours, Coach.

"What's got you smiling like that?"

Warmth blooms in my cheeks, but I try to maintain a calm expression. "Oh, just my lord and master checking in to make sure I slept."

"Lord and master," Kinsley mutters. "I never thought about it before, but your nickname for him is a little kinky. Maybe Ethan isn't the only one with a secret crush."

I roll my eyes even as my stomach flips. Kinsley's teasing about Ethan having a crush on me doesn't ring as false as it did before the kiss, and Ethan did seem almost jealous last night when Jake asked for my number. Why did I like it so much?

I don't have a crush on Ethan. He's not my type at all. Lately, I prefer guys like Jake, guys who make me feel at ease.

Then again, Ethan has been making me feel at ease recently. He's been so warm and self-deprecating with me. The time we spent together yesterday evening was some of the most fun I've had in months.

Another text appears on my screen, and this time, the hairs on my arms stand up.

This is now the second time in a few days that he's requested to talk to me. Unusual for him. Generally, these texts come about once a month, a reminder not to tell anyone what *didn't* happen. What does it mean?

I set my phone down with a thud, trying to push the anxiety aside. I don't give a fuck about him. I'll ghost him until the end of eternity.

* * *

Ethan

"So how is everything going with Lily?" Noah asks.

My eyes snap open. I lift my head from the cool window. The vibrations of the bus rumbling down the freeway always lull me into a state of hypnosis.

We just won a game against Sierra Valley—one of our toughest rivals. Normally, I'd be daydreaming about my performance, analyzing every route, every catch, every decision I made on the field.

It seems like all I can think about lately is a fiery girl with sparkling eyes. Every time, my stomach flutters and my breath catches.

It's silly. I'm like a junior high boy with a crush.

Goddamn that impulsive decision to kiss her. It's fucked up everything and made me fixate on her when I shouldn't be thinking this way about my best friend's little sister. I've been called by God to help her, damn it.

"She's doing great," I say. "We changed our approach. I've decided to become her sleep coach. She's barely sleeping four hours a night because she's so stressed about her grades."

Noah frowns incredulously. "Her sleep coach? What do you mean?"

"I helped her come up with a sleep ritual. She's going to wind down at night with a relaxing activity and testing a new sleep supplement. Next week, when we meet up, we'll see if it worked."

"You can't only work on her sleep, Ethan. She's got way more problems than just that. She has to improve her grades if she doesn't want to get kicked out of college."

I want to roll my eyes. Why does he have to be so hard on her? "She's not like you and me. She's the type of person who needs to tackle one problem at a time."

Noah's eyes narrow. "You seem to know a lot about her after one accountability session."

My face heats. Does he suspect my interest in Lily is more than just that of the older brother figure he expects me to be? Maybe I'm giving something away. My whole body responds to the mere thought of her. Can he see how much I'm drawn to her by the look in my eyes?

I try to push the thought away. I can't forget that I've been lying to Noah about the night Lily and I kissed. Guilt is making me paranoid.

"Believe it or not," I say, "Lily and I are becoming friends. She still teases me constantly." I smile, unable to help myself. "But we're able to laugh together."

Noah's eyes widen. "That's insane. I would have bet money you'd be ready to strangle her after one time meeting up with her. She's certainly never liked you."

A cold stone settles in my gut. I hate the idea that she's never liked me. Why did I have to be such a dick to her?

Maybe Brandon and Mariana were right that I was repressing my attraction. Maybe my refusal to acknowledge that I want her left me feeling restless and irritated, which made me lash out.

It doesn't matter. God has called me to help her, and that's what I'm going to do. I can hold these feelings inside. I have the self-control of a monk.

I scratch the back of my head. "Yeah, well, she's a pain, but we get along."

Noah's expression softens. "I'm glad you're getting along. There's no other guy I'd trust to be friends with my sister."

Guilt squeezes my chest. He wouldn't be saying that if he knew the full truth. I kissed his sister like I've never kissed anyone before.

What does that say about my integrity that I'm willing to lie by omission to save my own ego? Noah would most likely forgive me if I told him about the kiss. My fear is irrational. But he might not see me the same way again, and that thought is deeply unsettling.

Maybe my true fear is that I've never really known myself.

Chapter Nine

L^{ily}

My steps are light as I trot down the sidewalk. The sun dips below the horizon, draping the ocean in a breathtaking mix of pink and gold. A warm blanket of peace wraps around my heart. I haven't been this optimistic in months.

I'm making progress. I slept six hours last night—the longest I have in months, and it's all thanks to Ethan and his rigid sleep rituals.

He's been texting me daily, asking for me to recount the night before. Then he gives me a new ritual to try—like turning my phone off an hour before bed—with the commanding certainty of a doctor writing a prescription. It never fails to make me smile. He's such a stickler, and I never found it endearing until recently.

Whoever thought this would happen with Ethan of all people? I thought for sure his type-A energy would stress me out, but then again, I never expected him to be so sweet and self-depre-cating. He actually makes me laugh. When I'm in his presence, I

60

feel like the old me—the real me—instead of this stress ball with the constantly buzzing anxiety.

I'm actually looking forward to our check-in session this evening.

"Why haven't you texted me back?"

The voice slices through the air, making my whole body grow taut. I squeeze the strap of my messenger bag as I turn around, and there stands Mason under the flickering streetlight with that all-too-familiar scowl.

I'm at the front of the sorority house, which means he must have been waiting for me. Lurking.

"I've texted you a hundred times," he says, his jaw tight. "I don't understand why you're ignoring me."

Really, you disgusting slug? You raped me.

Why does even the thought of the word "rape" make me want to wince? It wasn't my fault. I know this, and yet that doesn't stifle the burning shame in my chest that tries to claw its way up my throat.

I should have known better. I never should have gotten drunk and put myself under his power. Now, I'm suffering the consequences. I've become a ghost of my former self.

The worst part is he insists he never raped me, and he's here to berate me once again. To make me promise I'll never tell anyone.

As if I ever would. No one would believe me if I did. I've learned enough from my research about how difficult rape is to prove, especially when the rapist is someone close to you. Someone you've already had sex with.

I take a deep breath. "I haven't responded to any of your texts in months. Why do you care now?"

His dark eyes narrow. "Noah's been weird with me lately. I feel like he knows something."

Rage flares suddenly, like dry leaves catching fire. "What do you think he knows, Mason?" I raise my chin. "If nothing happened, there's nothing to tell, right?"

His expression grows hesitant for a moment, but then he

takes a step in my direction. I flinch, and he must see it, because his eyes flash. "You'd better not have told anyone what you *think* happened. My whole football career could be over."

A chill runs down my spine. This is exactly how he acted the morning after he raped me. I told him the story, giving him the benefit of the doubt since he was so mindlessly drunk and maybe didn't remember. I could see in his eyes that he did remember, but he scoffed the whole thing off. Said I wasn't clear that I didn't want sex.

Except I told him to stop. Over and over again. I told him, and he only gripped my arms tighter.

Telling him the story from my point of view only enraged him. He hovered over me as he told me I could ruin his life if I kept saying what I was saying. He used his size to intimidate me, and his gall left me breathless. What about *my* life? And how did he not see the irony of being so violently committed to his innocence?

My smile feels like a sneer. "I don't give a shit about your football career, or should I say your non-existent chances of making it to the NFL."

His body grows utterly still, and his eyes grow almost wild. He didn't like that. Why did I say it? Why am I taunting a man who's prone to violence?

I inhale an unsteady breath. "I just want you to go away. We don't need to talk about this anymore. You don't have to worry about my 'crying rape', as you called it, so—"

He lunges toward me, wrapping his fingers around my wrists with a bruising force. A scream rips from my throat, raw and instinctual. I try to wrench away, but he squeezes my wrists tighter.

The world around me blurs as if I'm sinking underwater. I try to retreat into that foggy, dim recess of my mind where his touch can't reach me. Just like I did that night.

It only works for a moment. His hot breath against my forehead pulls me into the present world, to where my heart is fluttering like a bird .

"Shut the fuck up," he whispers through clenched teeth. "Did you not notice we're in public? You're 'crying rape' right the fuck now."

Crying rape. It's like the words alone will summon a firing squad, when the truth is that no one cares what happens to a college girl who put herself in danger in a haze of drunkenness.

His grip on my wrists sends a slice of pain up my arms, but I refuse to cower. I raise my chin to look him in the eyes. "If you're so worried about your public image, maybe you should stop assaulting me."

His nostrils flare. "I'm not assaulting you."

I try to pull back, but his grip on my wrists only tightens.

"What the fuck are you doing, Mason?"

Ethan's voice booms from behind me, and relief washes through my veins. For the first time, I'm grateful that he apparently watches me like a hawk from his window.

Mason's head snaps up, his eyes filling with fear. He lets go of my wrists and takes several steps back. "We were just talking," he says, lifting both hands in the air.

A moment later, Ethan's huge form steps into my vision, stalking toward Mason. He stops inches away from his body, hovering over him like Mason did to me a moment ago. "Why the fuck were you grabbing her?" Ethan clips out.

"I didn't..." Mason flinches, and my fading panic must be making me hysterical, because I want to laugh. How is he planning to talk himself out of this one? Stern commander Ethan isn't going to let him get away with laying his hands on a woman.

Mason licks his lip. "I wasn't grabbing her that hard. Please don't tell... Noah wouldn't understand."

Ethan laughs caustically. "Yeah, I don't think he would understand. In fact, he might even tell Coach Rodriguez and get you suspended. Assuming I don't get to him first."

Mason's eyes flash. "You wouldn't do that. You need me."

Ethan snorts. "You're barely an upgrade from any of our backup quarterbacks. I think the team would do just fine without you."

Ooh, Mason doesn't like that. He takes a step toward Ethan, nearly grazing his chest.

Ethan widens his stance. God, he looks like a giant. Mason might be tall, but he's nowhere near as muscular as Ethan. Mason seems to feel the difference between them, because he takes a step back.

I wish it didn't delight me. Ethan doesn't need to save me. I could have kneed Mason in the balls.

Why didn't I? Somehow when he grabbed me, all the fear from that night flooded back into my body.

Goddamn it, when will I finally be over this?

Mason shuts his eyes. "Please don't say anything. To anyone."

Ethan huffs. "You think I'm going to lie to protect you, needle dick? After what I just saw, I'm tempted to break your fucking nose."

Mason's eyes grow huge, and an almost hysterical giggle bubbles from my chest. I shouldn't be laughing. I need to intervene soon if Ethan is serious about his threat. But I can't get over the fact that I just heard Ethan Harrington utter the words "needle dick."

"You could get kicked off the team for that." Mason's chest is puffed out as he stares up at Ethan, but he can't hide his fear. Even from several feet away, I see how his body trembles.

Ethan shrugs. "Nah. I don't think I would. I think if I told Coach you assaulted Noah's little sister, he'd thank me for punching you in the face."

When Ethan takes another step in Mason's direction, I snap into action. I march forward and grab his shoulder. The tension in his body vibrates under my hand. He jerks around to look at me, looking almost startled by my presence.

"Don't hit him." My voice is firm. "He's not worth it."

Ethan's face falls. "Lily, I saw what he did—"

"You're right. You *saw* it. But it happened to me. Don't try to fight my battles for me."

He shuts his eyes. "He's my teammate. I can't let him get away with this."

"But I'm not your teammate, and this is my business. I don't want you giving him any more fuel. He'll come back here and harass me again. Thank God none of my sisters saw what he did."

When footsteps pound on the sidewalk, both Ethan and I jerk our heads toward Mason. I want to laugh when I see he's practically jogging in the opposite direction.

"Fucking coward," Ethan mutters before raising his voice to say, "This isn't over, Mason."

Mason doesn't even turn his head.

"This *is* over," I say. "Let me deal with Mason."

Ethan turns to me, his eyes narrowing on his face. "Why would you care if your sorority sisters saw? I wish they did. They need to know what he's like so they can protect you from him when I'm not here." He shakes his head, his eyes growing unfocused. "I can't believe he grabbed you like that. I knew he was a dick but I never thought he'd—" His gaze snaps to my face. "Has he done something like this before?"

I open my mouth, but the words don't come.

Why can't I just admit that Mason's been violent before? I don't have to go into detail about the rape.

Yet even a vague explanation might make me cry, and holy fuck, I don't want to cry. The rape has wreaked enough havoc on my emotions, and Mason doesn't deserve my tears.

"Look." I raise my hands. "I don't want to go into detail, but suffice it to say that I've seen his temper before, and I don't trust—"

"Holy shit." Ethan's huge eyes are fixed on my wrists. He steps forward and grabs my arm. He rubs his thumb over the red welts on my skin. "Oh my God," he whispers.

With the utmost gentleness, he grabs my other wrist and lifts it up to examine it. When he's done, he shuts his eyes tightly, his breathing rapid. "I'm going to kill him." His voice is quiet.

Chilling.

"No, you're not," I grit out. "I just want Mason to go away and leave me alone."

And not just in real life. I want him to leave my head as well. I want to finally accept that I can't change what happened and move on with my life. I want to become the fun, free, wild Lily again.

Except this version of wild Lily won't trust men so easily.

"He *hurt* you." Ethan's jaw is so tight it looks like it might snap in two. "He can't get away with it. I won't allow it."

"It's not up to you what's allowed. This is *my* life, and I don't want any more trouble. Just think of what could happen if we tell people Mason grabbed me. You only *threatened* to punch him, but Noah doesn't have nearly as much self-control as you do. He might actually do it."

Ethan's mouth drops open. "Are you implying that we're not even going to tell Noah?"

"Of course not. He has to live with Mason."

"The fuck he does! He'd move out of that apartment in a second if he knew Mason hurt you. And I wasn't only talking about telling Noah. I think you need to go to the police, and I'll come with you. I was a witness."

Panic grips my chest. "Absolutely not. Are you not hearing me? I want to forget about this. I want to forget about Mason."

If we went to the police, eventually the whole campus would find out. Every football player on the Hawks is famous at Mission Hills. I'd be under the inspection of thousands of people. Everyone would be picking apart what really happened and pointing fingers at who they think is really to blame for Mason's assault charge. What if they decide a random girl who no one's heard of isn't worth losing their quarterback mid-season? What if they decide to blame me instead?

The thought makes me want to dry heave.

"Lily, this is a big deal. He put welts on your wrists. Why are you brushing this off?"

"I'm not brushing it off. I'm asking you to stop making it all about you."

His eyes grow pained. He looks like he wants to press me further, but then he takes a step back. "Alright, fine. I promise not to do anything right now, but—" his expression grows stern "—you and I are going to have a talk later."

I roll my eyes. "Fine."

He sighs. "Come inside the frat house. I'll get some ice packs for your wrists."

"They really don't hurt that much."

He scowls. "If you don't want me to go to the cops right the fuck now, you need to come inside and let me put some ice on your goddamn wrists. That's the deal I'm offering you. Take it or leave it."

My lips quirk. "I know you're a Christian who swears, but I don't think I've ever heard you do it this much, big guy."

His lips twist into a half smile. "Yeah? I'm fucking pissed off. Can you fucking tell?"

I snort. "Yes."

He raises both brows. "And the reason your damn wrists don't hurt is because of the goddamn adrenaline pumping through your veins. I know this, because I've sustained a lot of minor injuries during games. You need ice to make the swelling go down. Can you accept my goddamn expertise on this?"

"Yes," I say, smiling. "I'll let you get your goddamn fucking ice packs."

He smiles, and gratitude blooms in my chest. It warms me from the inside out, snuffing out the last vestiges of fear. Why did I never appreciate Ethan's protectiveness before now? He's like a warrior, fierce and steadfast.

It's hot, and it was never hot before. It always seemed

presumptuous and condescending. But this new scared Lily could use a protector. At least until she can get over this debilitating anxiety.

Chapter Ten

E^{than}

My hands are still shaking as I reach into the freezer and grab the ice pack. Fuck, I think my entire body is trembling.

I've never been so enraged in my life. Mason was squeezing Lily's wrists, staring into her eyes like he was ready to kill her.

And there she was, my fiery Lily, looking so scared and small, unable to defend herself. It seemed so unlike her. Even though he's bigger than her, I'd expect her to fight back more than she did. It's almost as if...

He's done something in the past. Something that put the fear of God in her.

This is what Kinsley was talking about. This is what she must suspect. Mason was violent with Lily. That's why she's been so withdrawn these last several months. That's why she can't sleep and her grades are suffering.

This is why God called me to help her. This is why I caught Mason when I did. It was blind luck that I happened to be looking out my window when he approached her. Though I suppose I have been looking out for her a lot recently.

I just have to convince her that she can trust me. That nothing bad is going to happen if she goes to the cops. I'll make sure Mason never lays a hand on her again, even if I have to watch her like a damn guard dog.

As I turn around to face her, I take a deep breath to calm myself. I can't let her see my simmering rage. Now is the time to start building her trust in me, to let her know I'm a safe place to lay her troubles.

I walk to where she stands by the counter. Her scent washes over me, sweet and floral. I blink a few times in an attempt to clear my head. "Alright, give me your right hand."

She holds out her small wrist with the red welts around it, and another rush of rage sizzles through my veins. Oh fuck. How will I ever stand face-to-face with Mason again without punching him in the face?

"You look like you're ready to murder someone," she says. "I told you it doesn't hurt, big guy."

When my gaze snaps to Lily's face, she's staring at me with an exasperated expression. Even in my anger, I find myself smiling.

Big guy.

She's invented a lot of nicknames for me over the years, especially when I've bossed her around. Grumplestiltskin, lord and master, and my recent favorite, her joy vacuum. But something about "big guy" tugs at my heart. It's softer and almost...affectionate.

She winces as I wrap the ice pack around her wrist and attach the Velcro. I frown. "You said it didn't hurt."

She wrinkles her nose. "It doesn't. I hate the cold. It feels terrible, like pins and needles. I'd rather use a heating pad."

I shake my head. "It needs to be iced. Heat could make it swell up even more."

She groans. "Who cares if it feels good?"

"Lily, let me do my job."

"Are you a doctor now?"

I look at her gravely. "No, I'm the joy vacuum, remember? It's my job to ensure your misery. You need to keep the ice pack on for five minutes and then switch to the other wrist so I can vacuum up the rest of the joy. I gotta be thorough."

She smiles, and the sight of it makes my heart flutter. "I can't believe I called you that. What a dick thing to say."

I laugh. "Yeah, you can be a dick sometimes, but I probably deserve it."

She shakes her head. "You don't. You're pretty selfless, and I wish I appreciated it more. I can't believe how much time you've spent helping me with my sleep, especially when you have so much on your plate."

Right. I'm selfless. That's why my accountability partner job evolved into daily texts about her sleep. Why I can't wait to get a response, even when the subject matter would be boring if I was texting with anyone else.

Not because the mere thought of her lights me up inside.

"Speaking of which," Lily starts, "should we go ahead and start our sleep coaching session early? We might as well since I'm already here."

"Sure, but we're not going to talk in the study. I want to get your mind off today. How about we watch a movie or something?"

The shock in her eyes makes my face heat. Did it sound like an excuse to her? Like I just want to spend an intimate evening with her and invented a reason to do it?

"I didn't even know you watch movies," she says.

Ah, so she thinks I don't know how to distract her, that because I'm so rigid in my routines, I don't know how to have fun. "I don't that often, but I'll watch whatever you pick from start to finish. I can even promise I won't do a single burpee. I hope you understand how difficult that'll be for me."

"No, no." She sets her hand on my arm. "You need to hit your burpee count for the day. I refuse to let you make such a grave sacrifice on my behalf."

Heat creeps into my cheeks. Clearly, Noah told her about how I make sure I get in a hundred burpees a day before bedtime. No wonder she's always thought I have a stick up my ass.

I do have a stick up my ass.

I clear my throat. "Alright, I'll head to the gas station and grab some snacks. What do you want?"

Her eyes grow huge. "Anything I want? Like Doritos and Reese's Peanut Butter Cups?"

"Sure."

Her smile grows mischievous. "And you'll eat them with me, right?"

I fight the urge to cringe. So many carbs.

But I refuse to have a stick up my ass tonight. I'm taking a day off from my exercise and diet protocol. "Sure, and I normally don't eat anything after six o'clock, especially not empty carbs. I'm laying down my life for you."

"A hero. Thank you for your service, Private Harrington."

I nod. "It's my honor to serve. Alright, anything to add to the list besides Reese's and Doritos?"

Her face lights up. "Oh, yes. Sour skittles and a fountain Dr. Pepper. It must be fountain with lots of ice, and I want the biggest size they have. I *do* mean the biggest size. If they have a sixty-four-ounce cup, you're getting it. Don't let me down, soldier."

I groan. "That will be just for you. Dr. Pepper has caffeine. I never drink caffeine this late."

"Oh, no." She winces dramatically. "What'll happen if you accidentally take a sip? Will I need to take you to the hospital?"

"No, we have a defibrillator in the first aid kit. You should be able to resuscitate me on your own."

Her smile fades, and what looks like surprise flashes in her eyes.

"What?" I ask.

She shakes her head slowly. "Why were you never like this before? Whenever I teased you... You just always seemed annoyed. I never thought you could be so...fun."

Fun. The word hits me like a jolt of electricity. Lily Greenwood thinks I'm fun.

With effort, I maintain a blank expression. "I was never that annoyed with you. This is just what my face looks like all the time. It's called resting joy vacuum."

She grins. "And what a handsome joy vacuum you are."

When she reaches out and pinches my cheek, heat shoots into my gut. Fuck, this isn't good. Even a playful touch from her sets my body on fire.

I'll need to sit on the other end of the couch when we watch our movie.

I take a step back. "Why don't you scroll through Netflix and pick out a movie? We'll be watching it in my room, because I have the biggest TV in the house. When you go upstairs, it's the first door on your right."

An almost naughty smile plays at her full lips. "Will I be the first girl to enter Ethan Harrington's sacred space?"

I snort. "I live in a damn frat house, Lily. So no, you won't be."

Though she is the first woman I've ever planned to spend an evening with alone in my bedroom, and the thought makes my stomach twist with nerves.

What am I afraid of? I'll never touch her again. My recent attraction to her might be messing with my head, but my self-control is stronger.

Chapter Eleven

E^{than}

I walk into my bedroom with a large bag under my arm and an ice-cold drink in my hand. When I glance at the couch, Lily is sitting with her gaze fixed on the TV. The ice pack is notably resting on the coffee table with drops of condensation forming around it.

My instinct is to tell her to put it on her left wrist, but that can wait. I don't want to remind her of what happened today when she looks so peaceful.

I stride over to the couch and set the bag on top of the coffee table. "Did you pick out a movie?"

"Not yet." A playful gleam appears in her eyes as I sit down beside her. "I've been trying to find something torturous for you —which, as you know, is my favorite pastime—but I have no idea where to start. First, I looked for a boring black and white French film, but then I thought you might like that. You're all about improving your mind, so maybe you like intellectual, artsy movies."

My stomach sinks at her words. I do strive to improve my mind, but it's never bothered me before. Until this moment, I've never felt so much like a stereotypical wellness gym rat.

Do I even have a favorite movie? I can't remember the last time I watched one all the way through. I usually spend my evenings looking at replays of our latest game, critiquing my own performance.

I try to smile, but it feels more like a grimace. "I can assure you that I don't spend the little time I have watching boring French movies. My favorite movie is *Remember the Titans*," I lie, choosing the only movie I've seen more than once.

Here I am, creating a personality to please a girl who claims I don't have one.

What has gotten into me?

"I hate sports movies," Lily says with a frown. "I've seen every single one, thanks to Noah, and they're all the same. Will they win the big game of the season? Spoiler alert, they will, and I'll have to suffer through all their whining until they finally pull it off. And the romance will suck, because the female lead's life will completely revolve around the star athlete." She cringes. "There is no universe in which I'd pick a sports movie."

"What would be the point of picking one? Your goal is to torture me."

Her eyes probe into mine as she sets her hand on my arm. The small touch sends a ripple of electricity over my skin.

Fuck, I really can't let her touch me. I'll need to discreetly scoot myself to the other end of this couch when she isn't looking

"I just thought of a movie," she says, "and I hate to admit it, but I'm really hoping it won't be torture for you. It's my favorite of all time."

I lean toward her, genuinely curious. I've known her for over two years, but since I've kept my distance, I don't know much about her. "What is it?"

"*Jurassic Park.*"

I chuckle, mostly at the delight in learning something I never would have predicted. "*That's* your favorite movie?"

She scowls. "How dare you laugh? It's a perfect movie. Two hours long without a single boring moment."

Warmth fills my chest. "Without a single boring moment." How quintessentially Lily. Of course, *Jurassic Park* would be her favorite movie.

What is it about this wild girl that calls to something deep inside me? Is it because she's my polar opposite? If I'm a joy vacuum, she's the sunshine that warms every shadow.

What the fuck? What a sappy thought. My recent fixation with her is making me crazy.

I clear my throat. "You'd better start the movie soon if you want me to stay awake the whole time."

She scoffs. "Try falling asleep during the T-Rex chase scene. I dare you."

Hours later, we're sitting on the couch with empty bags littered over the coffee table. Tiny crumbs are scattered over the wood. My hands have been itching to pick up the trash and wipe down the table, but Lily hasn't even glanced at it. I doubt she ever thinks about cleaning during her leisure time. She's not wired the way I am.

I won't clean it until after she leaves. I'm letting go, which apparently means resisting my instinct to wipe up chip crumbs.

Epic music plays over the stream of credits drifting up the screen. Lily hasn't acknowledged that the movie is over. In fact, her breathing is soft and rhythmic. Hasn't it been that way for a while now?

I twist around and see that her face is resting against the arm of the couch. When I lean forward, I see her eyes are closed and her mouth is open.

Holy shit. She's asleep. Sound asleep by the looks of it.

My stomach flips over. I stand up from the couch as quietly as

I can, exhilaration pumping through my veins. This is a big deal. A really big deal.

Or maybe I'm making too much of this. With as little sleep as she's been getting recently, she was bound to pass out eventually from sheer exhaustion.

So why do I feel like a king?

She told me she hasn't been able to sleep because of anxiety, and I'm now almost certain it has something to do with Mason. I was somehow able to make that anxiety go away, even after he grabbed her wrists today.

I think she's starting to trust me.

I'm pulled back into the present when a door slams, and loud voices from downstairs filter into my room.

Apprehension jolts within me as I glance at Lily. Her fiery hair spills over the side of the couch like a blanket. That full mouth of hers is wider now, and a faint snoring sound echoes through the room. It's fucking adorable.

I'll be damned if I let anyone wake her.

I rush out of my room and down the stairs. When I get to the bottom floor, a group of my frat brothers are standing around our beer pong table.

"Keep your voices down," I command as softly as I can. "I have a girl over, and she's sleeping."

When their eyes grow huge, I want to wince. I wish I had thought more before I phrased it that way.

"You have a girl over?" Damian nearly shouts, and I shush him. "Is Ethan finally getting laid?"

"I hate to tell you this, Ethan," Aiden says, "but if she's asleep, you're doing something wrong."

I roll my eyes. "Or maybe I did something right, Aiden. Maybe you've never seen a girl sleep after sex because you don't know where the clitoris is located."

When "Oh's" break out throughout the room, I want to kick myself. What possessed me to clap back at Aiden? My brothers' relentless teasing over my virginity has never bothered me before.

But this is Lily, and somehow, the idea of boring her to sleep during sex doesn't sit well, which is stupid. I would never, *ever* have sex with her.

"Do not repeat what I just said," I command the room. "This girl is...like a little sister to me."

The words taste like ash in my mouth. I wish I hadn't even said them, but it's not fair to Lily to have people thinking we slept together because of my careless words.

And I wouldn't want it getting back to Noah.

When the guys have finally quieted down to my liking, I make my way back to my bedroom. Lily is in the exact same position as I left her.

Shit. Her hands are curled up underneath her head, and she's probably so exhausted she doesn't even feel the pain in her wrists. I can't let her sleep like that much longer.

I should move her to my bed. It could wake her, but it would be worth the risk.

You want to hold her, Ethan. Don't lie to yourself.

It doesn't matter what I want. Even if my hands are twitching with the need to touch her, this is about what she needs. Her wrists will probably be blue and purple by tomorrow, and I can't let her injure them further.

After bending down, I carefully slip one arm under her knees and the other around her shoulders. She stirs slightly, murmuring something incoherent. A smile rises to my lips.

I lift her gently and pull her against my chest. Her little breaths tickle my neck, and the warmth of her body seeps into mine.

Fuck, this feels good. Why does it have to feel so good?

When I reach my bed, I lay her down and tuck my comforter around her. She curls up instinctively and shifts around until she's lying on her side.

Unable to help myself, I reach out and stroke her hair from her face with the lightest of touches. Fuck, it's so soft. Even silkier than it looks.

I stand here for a long while staring at her, my feet feeling leaden. What is this strange prickling at the back of my neck? The sight of her snuggled in my bed is unsettling in a way I can't quite articulate. My chest aches as an electrifying tingle runs over my skin.

Then it hits me.

I want to be in that bed with her. In the moment, it feels like I'd sacrifice everything for it, including my whole religion.

Shit. Where did that blasphemous thought come from?

Chapter Twelve

L ily

A deep voice pulls me from the darkness. When my eyes crack open, the room is full of bright morning light. Why are the walls gray? The white crown molding on the edge of the ceiling doesn't look familiar.

Where the hell am I? The last thing I remember is watching *Jurassic Park* with...

Ethan.

I jerk up, my eyes darting around the room until I find the source of the voice. Ethan is sitting on the couch with his phone to his ear.

"Did I wake you?" He winces. "Sorry, I tried to keep my voice down. Brandon, can I call you back? Sleeping beauty just woke up."

Warmth unfurls in my belly at his words. *Sleeping beauty.* What an adorable nickname.

But it's all so bizarre. Why is Ethan acting like this is no big deal? I passed out on his couch and woke up in his bed, and now he's telling his pastor brother about it like it's the most normal occurrence in the world. Golden boy Ethan just had a woman sleep over, and he's completely nonchalant about it.

Ethan says goodbye to Brandon and sets his phone on the coffee table. He marches over to the bed with a satisfied smirk on his face. "You slept twelve hours."

My head jerks back. "*Twelve* hours? What time is it?"

"Nine thirty. I've already worked out, showered, and finished a paper. It wasn't easy. I had to use earplugs to drown out your snoring."

I lift my hand to my mouth. "I snore?"

He grins. "A little bit. I didn't really have to use earplugs, but I couldn't miss out on an opportunity to embarrass you."

"If it were possible to embarrass me, I think passing out on your couch and stealing your bed would be enough. How did I even get here?"

A brush of pink appears on his cheekbones. "I carried you to my bed, and I slept on the couch. I figured..." His gaze falls to the floor. "I wanted to make sure you stayed asleep since—you know —it was a big deal."

He carried me while I was asleep, and I let him do it. My body didn't jerk awake at the unfamiliar touch. Whoever thought I'd be comfortable with a man holding me in my sleep, even innocently?

A quietness settles in my heart. This is Ethan. He might be a pain in my ass, but I trust him more than anyone I know.

It's also hilarious that he put me to bed like a daddy.

"You carried me?" I suck in my lips. "That's so cute."

His smile grows rueful. "It was pretty cute of me, actually. I even tucked you in."

God, he's sweet. How did I never see this side of him until this last week?

"Well, this was a miracle, Ethan. Seriously. I feel like a new person."

I feel like the old me, I would say if I could.

His expression grows serious. "I think we figured out something key last night. You need a change of environment to help you get into the habit of sleeping again."

"How do you expect me to do that? I can't switch rooms with one of the girls in the house just like that." I snap my fingers. "Our rent is based on the size of our rooms."

He stares at me for a long moment. "You should sleep here. In my room."

Shock vibrates through my body. "Are you out of your mind?"

He shakes his head decisively. "I was just talking to my brother about this, and he agrees with me. If you were able to sleep in this room for a full night once, you should be able to do it again. Sleep works that way. Your body learns to associate an environment with sleep or lack of sleep. Which is why you're having a hard time sleeping in your room. Your body has learned that you can't sleep there."

I frown. "Well then, how will I ever be able to sleep in my room again?"

"Hopefully, by sleeping here for a bit, you'll break the association, which means you'll need to stay here for a while. Let's say a week."

My head grows fuzzy. An image comes to mind of lying in this bed with Ethan's big arms around me.

I swallow. "Where will you sleep?"

"I'll take the downstairs couch."

I snort. "In a frat house. You'll never sleep a wink. No, we're not doing this."

He walks over to the bed and sits beside me. "I really think we should, Lily. Don't worry about me. I work my body to death during workouts and practice. I sleep like the dead."

My head grows fuzzy. This is crazy talk. What would it say about my mental health if I agreed to this? I'm such a mess that I have to steal someone's entire room? No. I refuse to let Mason have that kind of power over me.

"I'll just try Ambien again," I say. "I haven't tried it in months and—"

Ethan groans. "Why do you think it would work now if it didn't before? The one thing that's worked so far is sleeping in my room. If you don't try it, it's because you're a quitter."

I snort out a laugh. "Very insightful, Coach."

"It's true." His tone is surly.

I let out a heavy sigh. "Alright, fine. I'll try it for a week, but I'm not making you sleep on the couch downstairs. If we do this, you sleep in your bed, and I'll take the couch downstairs."

He looks at me incredulously. "You think I'm letting you sleep in the main room of a house full of dudes? Dudes who get drunk almost every night? Absolutely not."

Heat blooms in my tummy at the vehemence in his tone. He's always been overprotective of me, but it never turned me on until that kiss.

"Then I can sleep on the couch in here," I say. "I'm not taking your bed."

His gaze drifts to the couch in the corner of the room, his cheeks darkening. Is he imagining what it would be like to share a room with me?

"If you're comfortable being in the same room," Ethan says, his voice strained, "then you take my bed, and I'll sleep on the couch."

I bite my bottom lip. "What will we tell your brothers?"

He snorts. "They all have girls sleep over all the time. Some of them have girlfriends practically living with them." His expression grows stern. "But I'd rather you stay in my room as much as you can, especially at night. There's always a party here, and I don't want any of them getting handsy with you."

It takes everything within me to keep from laughing. He knows for a fact that I've been to plenty of frat parties, including here. In fact, over a year ago, I fell in the toilet and took all my wet clothes off. Several of his frat brothers have seen me naked.

Ethan didn't like that. He didn't like it at all. Aside from yesterday when Mason grabbed me, I don't think I've ever seen him so angry.

I clear my throat. "Deal."

His whole face lights up like fireworks in a dark sky. Wow. He's really happy that I said yes. The guy who can't stand me is excited to share his personal space with me for an entire week. My stomach does a little turn. What does it mean?

He reaches out his hand to shake mine. "I expect a commitment of a full week from you." His voice is stern. "That's the deal."

I smile lazily as I wrap my hand around his and shake. "Your wish is my command, oh lord and master."

He grips my hand tightly as an unreadable emotion flickers in his eyes. "You haven't called me that in a while." His voice is husky. "I've actually kind of missed it. It's such a Lily thing to say."

My breath quickens. He's *missed* it? He's only become this softer version of himself over the last week.

Is it possible I misread him? What if he enjoyed my teasing from the very beginning—like Kinsley has always thought—and I just couldn't see it?

Ethan lets go of my hand and stands up. "Okay, this is what we're going to do." He paces the floor in front of me. "I'll plan a whole sleep routine for you, but this will be much more elaborate than what I've had you do this last week. We'll go all out. Chamomile tea and melatonin. Strict bedtimes and times to wake up, and I'll have you do activities during the day that'll help you sleep at night, like going for a run—"

"Oh, fuck no." I shake my head sharply. "No running. If you're planning on working me that hard, the deal is off."

He scowls. "We just shook on it."

"We sure did. You might take your promises seriously, but I don't. Not when they ruin my life."

A soft smile tugs at his lips. "Running would ruin your life?"

"I can only assume it would. I've never tried it for exercise, because it looks awful and un-fun. I get my workouts by walking on campus, thank you very much. And if that's not enough, I'll die early. At least I'll go out happy."

He chuckles. "You're a truly ridiculous person."

I inhale a sharp breath. Why was his voice so caressing? He called me ridiculous as if it's an endearment. As if he loves that I'm ridiculous. A shiver of delight runs down my spine, and my cheeks flush. How nice would it be to find a man who cherishes my frivolousness?

It can't be Ethan. He might be a little bit attracted to me, but he'd never want me long term. Even if Noah were okay with a relationship between us, Ethan wouldn't date a woman who isn't a Christian. From what Noah has told me, Ethan only ever plans to date his future wife when he meets her.

Bizarre.

How could I ever be with a man like that anyway? It would be like dating an alien.

"Your wrists are bruised." Ethan's serious voice startles me. "Can you let me take a look at them?"

My skin prickles at the reminder of yesterday. Fuck, why didn't I fight harder? It's humiliating that Ethan had to come to my rescue.

"Sure." My voice is small.

Ethan nods before sitting down beside me. He picks up my wrists one by one and examines them closely, rubbing them gently with his thumbs. His fingers are big and rough, sending electric currents up my arms.

When he's done, he sets my hands gently on my lap. "They aren't as bad as I expected, but I want you to ice them again before you leave. You're going to need to head to your sorority house to pack a bag for the week. I don't want you stepping foot in that house while we're trying this experiment."

I nod. "Got it, Coach."

"We also need to talk about what happened with Mason. I promised you a reprieve, but I'm not going to let it go after what I saw him do. If you don't want me to go straight to the cops when you go get your stuff, you need to give me a damn good reason. Right now."

My stomach plummets to the floor. "I already told you why." My voice is strained. "I don't want to rock the boat. I just want Mason to leave me alone."

"Yep, and you could easily solve that with a restraining order. You're going to need to do better than that."

His cold, commanding tone raises my hackles. He sounds like the Ethan I used to know. The one I couldn't stand.

I raise my chin and look him in the eyes. "It should be enough that I've asked you not to do it. This is what *I* need. This is how *I* want to deal with what happened. If you can't respect that, then maybe we shouldn't hang out anymore. I can tell Noah to go to hell with this whole accountability partner thing."

"Lily." His tone is pleading. "What Mason did was wrong. Reprehensible. He needs to face consequences."

"But *I* don't. I've dealt with enough of Mason's bullshit. I don't need him going on social media and posting about the crazy bitch who falsely accused him of assaulting her."

He raises both hands in the air. "But I saw it. I can back you up."

"He'd still insist I'm crazy. That man is a moron." I shake my head. "I don't want any more drama. I just want to forget about him."

Ethan sighs heavily.

"And you can't tell Noah either."

His eyes grow huge. "I can't believe you. Noah is my best friend. He would kill me if he knew his sister was assaulted and I didn't tell him about it."

"Yes, because he's a patriarchal tyrant who thinks he owns his sister."

Ethan's eyes grow hard. "That's not something I can agree to in good conscience. All I can give you is a promise that I won't tell him for the rest of the week while you're sleeping here. After that, you and I are going to have to have another talk. I'll give you another reprieve while we get your sleep in order, but that's it. I can't keep lying to him forever."

"Fine."

He nods once. "Can I ask you one more question?"

I swallow, and an ominous chill runs down my spine. "Sure."

He opens his mouth and then closes it, as if searching for the right words. "You told me yesterday that you've seen Mason's temper. What does that mean exactly?"

My heart jumps into my throat, and repressed words scream to get out.

Tell him, Lily. You don't have to go into detail, but you can give him a small glimpse of what Mason did. Ethan already knows he's violent.

I can't do it. The thought of telling even a sanitized version of what Mason did makes me want to dry heave.

"Just that I've seen him...lose his temper," I finally say.

Ethan's eyes narrow. "But he never hurt you before?"

I hesitate for a moment. "No."

Ethan nods once, and I release the breath I've been holding.

No. Such a simple word. One of the first we learn as babies, and uttered probably a million times before we die.

Yet I think I'll always remember saying it this time. It's as if when it left my mouth, a bit of my soul slipped away with it.

Chapter Thirteen

Ethan

Water cascades over my skin, washing away the grime and sweat of the game. We nearly lost tonight, all because of my lack of focus.

I'm almost never distracted during a game. Usually, when I enter the field, even the roar of the crowd fades into the ether. I'm locked in. I know the match up. I've watched footage of the opposing team. It's time to let my body react to whatever happens on the field. Nothing outside of the game has any power over my instincts.

That wasn't the case tonight.

My quarterback and I are supposed to be in perfect sync, reading the defense together, anticipating each other's moves, and executing our plays with precise timing and trust.

But the only way to stifle my rage against Mason was to retreat into my head and pretend there was someone else behind that helmet. It took all my willpower, and I had nothing left over for the game.

There was a moment in the locker room before the game when Mason shot me a look. One that said if I tell anyone what he did, he'd make me regret it.

I wanted to march right up to Coach Rodriguez's in front of our whole team and tell him what I witnessed yesterday. I wanted everyone to know what a despicable human being Mason is, to publicly humiliate him.

I couldn't. Lily made me promise not to.

A promise that's splitting me into two people. One who's determined to earn her trust. To make her feel safe with me and get her to confide in me about her troubles. My gut tells me there's much more to her history with Mason than she told me this morning.

The other is ready to kill Mason.

"Hey," Noah says as I make my way to my locker. "You pulled through in the end. That catch was clutch."

Normally, his encouragement when I fuck up irritates me. I don't need to be coddled. I have no problem owning my mistakes. But I don't even care about the game tonight. Lily is the only thing that matters right now.

"I need to talk to you about something," I say.

"Sure," Noah says with a questioning frown on his face.

Fuck, I wish I could tell him the real thing that's troubling me. He'd kill me if he knew I was keeping a secret this big.

I bend down to lace up my shoes, not wanting to see his face. To be tempted to let the whole story spill from my lips. "Lily fell asleep on my couch last night. She was so exhausted, she just passed out. I let her sleep over for the night."

"She fell asleep while you were tutoring her?" He chuckles. "That sounds like Lily." He tilts his head as he examines my face. "I don't mind if she slept at your house, bro. I trust you more than anyone. I know you would never...do anything with her."

Guilt churns my gut. "I know, but that's not all. I'm going to let her sleep in my bed for a week."

When his eyes widen, my face heats. "I won't be sharing it with her, obviously."

"Obviously," he scoffs. "But still... Giving her your bed seems a little extreme."

It does. In fact, it never sounded crazy until this moment. Are my intentions pure, or do I just want Lily around all the time. Seeing her cuddled up in a bed that belongs to me?

I can't deny the dark possessiveness that started heating my blood the second she agreed to my proposition. Somehow, the mere thought of her sleeping in my bed for a week makes her feel like she belongs to me.

Mine. That's the word that comes to mind when I imagine that red hair cascaded over my pillow.

Jesus, help me get these feelings under control.

I clear my throat. "It's a new tactic we're trying. She told me she hasn't been sleeping for months. I think it's the whole reason she's not able to concentrate on her studies. If this works, I might not need to be her accountability partner anymore."

"Ah." Noah smiles. "So you're hoping to clear out your schedule. I'm sorry if it was too much of a time commitment."

I grit my teeth at his implication. Does he think I don't give a shit about Lily, that I only agreed to help her in order to please him? "It's just an experiment. If it doesn't work, we'll go back to the original plan."

He nods. "It's fine with me. I'm not even sure why you're telling me. You not worried that I'd be suspicious of your intentions, are you?"

I want to flinch. No, I'm not worried about that. He has more faith in me than I deserve.

A figure approaches us, making the hairs on my arms stand up. Even without seeing his face fully I know who it is, and I clench my hands into fists.

Mason. He was probably eavesdropping to make sure I wasn't telling Noah anything. When I glance up, he's examining Noah's face. He must like what he sees, because his tense face relaxes into a smug smile. "Rough game, Ethan." He shakes his head. "That drop in the fourth. Brutal."

"It was an off night," I say.

Because of you, dipshit. Because I know exactly who you are, and I'm powerless to do anything about it.

Mason leans against the locker beside me. "I wouldn't want a scout seeing me miss an easy pass."

Noah scoffs as he marches over to his locker and yanks a jacket out. "None of the scouts give a shit what you do out there. They come for Ethan." Noah turns to me, smirking. "Ready to go?"

I nod and start walking alongside Noah, but Mason steps out in front of us. "You seem really wound up, Ethan. Is something on your mind?"

The challenge in his eyes is unmistakable. Even as dense as he is, he's probably figured out that I'm not going to speak about what happened, and he's trying to exert power over me. Just like he did with Lily yesterday.

The bruises on her wrists flash into my mind. She has such small, delicate wrists, like the stems of a flower.

He crushed them. Turned them mottled and blue.

God, help me to control myself. Stop me from hitting him.

When I don't respond, Mason smirks. "Maybe you need to release some of that tension. It might help if you finally pop that cherry."

"Really helpful advice." Noah takes a step toward Mason. "Maybe someday Ethan will thank you by sending you Super Bowl tickets. No way you'll be able to afford them when you're selling life insurance."

When Mason's jaw clenches, I reach out and set my hand on Noah's shoulder, pulling him toward the locker room exit. "Great talk, Mason," I say. "Have the night you deserve."

Except he won't have the night he deserves, because that motherfucker deserves to be in jail.

As Noah and I make our way out of the locker room, he turns

to me. "I'm moving out of my apartment, dude. I can't fucking stand him."

I open my mouth, but nothing comes out. If I say one more word, I'll tell him everything.

He hurt your sister. He hurt her, and someday, I'll make him pay. I just have to move heaven and earth to get Lily to trust me first.

Chapter Fourteen

L ily

The door opens with a creak, and Ethan steps inside his bedroom, his big body so languid and graceful after what was probably a grueling game. I never go to their games anymore, determined as I am to avoid Mason. But I used to go fairly often, and even with my ignorance about football, I could see what a marvel Ethan is on the field.

He turns to where I sit on the couch, and his whole face brightens. My tummy flutters like it does every time he gives me this look. He always seems so...delighted with me now.

"What are you reading?" he asks.

I set my book on my lap. "*Atomic Habits*. A book that screams Ethan Harrington. I'm almost wondering if you wrote it, and—" I glance at the cover "—James Clear is your secret pen name."

His lips quirk. "Why the hell would you pick that one up?"

"It was all I could find. You don't have anything but productivity books."

He frowns. "You should have brought books from your house when you packed your bag. If you want, I can run over there and ask Kinsley to grab one for you."

I shake my head, though his thoughtfulness warms me. "This is good. It'll bore me to sleep."

He crosses his arms over his chest. "You won't need to be bored to fall asleep. I have a plan."

He looks so adorably stern that I want to kiss him. Damn him for vowing never to do that again.

"Tell me your plan."

Without answering, he walks to the gym bag he set by the door when he came in. After unzipping it, he pulls out a stick lighter and a box of some kind. "I bought candles on the way home," he says. "No more overhead lights."

I hum. "Romantic. Are you trying to seduce me, Mr. Harrington?"

He shoots me a bland expression that tells me he's fighting an eyeroll. "The opposite. I'm trying to put you to sleep."

After opening the plastic box, he pulls out a purple candle. As he moves around the room, he places candles on the kitchenette, his desk, and the coffee table, lighting them with quick, sure movements. The flickering flames add a warm glow to the room.

Then he turns off the lights, and I can hardly see a thing.

"This is too dark. I won't be able to read."

"Good. You'll be ready for bed sooner."

I groan as he marches toward the door. "I'll be right back," he says before disappearing.

While he's gone, I quickly grab my phone from the coffee table in front of me. I'm surprised he didn't take it away when he lit the candles. He already nagged me via text this past week that I'm not allowed to use my phone an hour before bed unless it's for reading and I dim the brightness.

When I swipe the screen, my breath catches. I have a text from Jake.

> Jake: I'm at a party a few streets down from
> your sorority. Any chance you can stop by and
> say hi?

Well, well. It took a week, but he finally texted me. Maybe the shy guy is finally ready to make a move.

Why isn't my stomach flipping over? I've had a crush on him for weeks. He's such a contrast to Mason, so mild-mannered and with a calmness I probably would have found boring months ago but now puts me at ease.

I'm not as excited as I thought I'd be. I'm not even disappointed that I have to tell him no. My domineering coach would never allow me to go to a party when he's trying to help me train myself to sleep.

Somehow, the thought of spending a quiet night with Ethan sounds much better than going to a party with Jake.

I don't have time to contemplate that thought further when Ethan strides into the room and sets a steaming coffee mug on the table in front of me. "Chamomile tea," he says before placing a small pill next to a glass of water. "And melatonin. Drink the tea now and take this right before bed."

I keep my head down so that he can't see my amusement at his commanding tone. After nodding, I reach for the mug. Warmth seeps into my hands as I take a sip.

Ethan's gaze shifts to my phone lying on my lap . Without a word, he grabs it and heads toward his desk. "I thought you already put this away. I told you no phone before bed. I'm putting this in my drawer."

"Wait, I need to send a text first." I reach out my hand. "It's Jake."

Ethan whips around, his eyes wide. "The guy from the coffee shop?"

"Yeah, the one I told you I like."

He stiffens, his jaw clenching. For a moment, he stares at me as if in indecision, but then he drops the phone into the drawer and shuts it with a snap. "You can text him back in the morning."

I stare at him, fighting a smile. His shoulders are rigid, and his hard gaze is fixed on my face.

Maybe I wasn't imagining it in the coffee shop. I think he really is jealous.

The thought sends a rush of heat through my veins. What if Ethan's overprotectiveness was always somewhat rooted in jealousy? It seems so odd that he would form a sudden attraction to me after one angry kiss. Maybe he's always wanted me, and he fought his attraction.

And what about me? Did I delight in provoking him because deep down, I wanted his attention? The way he looks at me now, with his iconic stern intensity, makes heat pool in my tummy.

Without another word, Ethan grabs a book from his desk and sits down beside me. His scent washes over me, fresh and clean with a hint of citrus.

I've always loved the way he smells. Even on the sidelines after a game—when he was sweaty—his scent had an undeniable earthy appeal. That has to be attraction. Liking someone's scent is such a primal thing, a deep, instinctual pull that defies logic.

To distract myself from these unsettling thoughts, I glance at the book in his hands. Oh my God, it's a Bible.

How adorable. The golden boy reads his Bible at night before bed.

"Is it interesting?" I ask, fighting a smile. "I've never read it."

He lets out a long sigh. "I wish I could say it was. I read through the whole thing every year, and there are some good stories. But most of it is...such a slog. I feel like a bad Christian, especially compared to my brother. He finds this whole book fascinating."

"Well, you're not a pastor like your brother. I'm sure God will forgive you. At least you're reading it, which is more than I can say for most Christians I know."

"I read it every night before bed, no matter what." He looks up at me, his smile lazy. "That's about as much as God can expect from a brainless gym rat like me, huh?"

I narrow my eyes. "If you're referring to my speech about your brand of asshole, I never called you brainless. The exact opposite. I said you were an *intellectual* gym rat."

His smile grows. "When it comes to gym rats, I don't think there's much of a difference. Not when all we care about is working out and taking supplements, which you also accused me of. Don't try to deny it. You were ridiculing me. As usual..." He reaches out and touches my nose with the tip of his finger. "Sassy girl."

I gasp, and the words hang in the air between us. *Sassy girl.* It's so different from other names he's called me in the past—irresponsible, reckless—and I wasn't imagining the warmth and softness in his voice. Why else would he be staring at me right now with unfathomably dark-blue eyes?

A charged silence follows, and I suddenly become hyperaware of his proximity. Is it just my imagination, or is he closer than he was a moment ago? His thigh is now pressed against mine, the warmth of his skin seeping through my pajama pants. The hairs on my arms stand on end.

Ethan shifts slightly, his breath brushing against my cheek, making me shiver. For a split second, his eyes flick to my lips before he pulls back. His gaze returns to his Bible, but his jaw is clenched.

"You have another half hour to read, and then it's lights out," he says, his voice a touch hoarser. "Or candles out, I should say."

I swallow, heat creeping into my cheeks. How silly that I thought he was going to kiss me again. He promised he never would. It doesn't matter if we've always been secretly attracted to each other, because it doesn't change anything.

I'm his best friend's little sister, and he only dates to marry.

"Yes, Coach," I say, pleasantly surprised at how even my voice sounds.

Chapter Fifteen

E^{than}

I love watching her brush her teeth.

She dances around the small kitchenette in my room with a frazzled energy. Her red hair is pulled up in a high bun that bobs back and forth with every fierce brush.

I have to stop myself from chuckling, not wanting to swallow my own toothpaste. She's so unapologetically herself. Even when brushing her teeth, she's bubbly and vivacious.

After only thirty seconds, Lily leans forward, spits into the sink, and grabs a towel to pat her face dry.

"That wasn't two minutes," I say, trying to sound stern but failing to hide the amusement in my voice.

Lily rolls her eyes dramatically, tossing the towel onto the counter. "Do you actually time yourself brushing your teeth?"

"I do. And I timed you. What else would you expect from a joy vacuum?"

"Ethan, stop. You're making me feel sorry for you." She steps closer and pokes me in the ribs. Her touch sends a jolt through me. As I watch her make her way over to my bed in those Spiderman pajama pants with her oversized Hawks T-shirt, my chest swells with an emotion I can't quite name.

We just got ready for bed together, and there was something so natural about it, like we've been doing it for years.

What is it about this girl that makes my heart so light?

It's as if she's a breath of fresh air, clearing away the cobwebs of my self-imposed constraints. When I'm with her, I find myself laughing more, relaxing into the moment instead of worrying about what comes next.

Strange, since she always used to drive me crazy.

Then again, I never allowed myself to be this close to her. Something about her always felt dangerous, like if I gave in to her energy, I'd lose control, be swept away in her whirlwind.

She crawls into my bed, the flickering candlelight casting soft shadows on her face. She pulls the covers up around her before nestling into the pillows. Possessiveness clenches my gut, along with a primal urge to crawl into that bed with her.

It's probably left over from the heat of jealousy that swept through my body when she told me she got a text from Jake. I couldn't help wondering what it was about. Were they flirting? Did he ask her on a date?

I don't want to think about it, so I distract myself by walking around the room and blowing out each candle one by one. The space gradually darkens, and the shadows grow longer until only the soft glow of the last candle remains.

I take a deep breath and blow out the final one, plunging the room into darkness. The only light now is the faint glow from the streetlights outside filtering through the curtains.

What would it be like to share the darkness with her? The whole world would be heat and skin and her delicious scent. My chest swells again, but the feeling behind it no longer eludes me.

Longing. There's no other word for it.

And there's nothing that can be done about it. She's off-limits, and I'm saving myself for my future wife.

I let out a deep sigh as I make my way to the couch. It's so tiny that I have to curl up, bending my legs to fit. I'm in for a long night of restless sleep, just like last night. It's okay, even if my physical and mental clarity suffer for it over the next week. Helping Lily is the greater good.

Blankets rustle on the other end of the room. "Ethan," Lily says, "there's no way you're sleeping like that."

"I'm fine. I slept here last night."

"Did you sleep well?"

I fight the urge to groan. I'm not going to lie to her, but I can evade the question. "It's only for a week."

She snorts. "You're what, six-four? You can't fit on that thing. We're switching."

"No, we're not. And if you don't stop mouthing off to your coach, I'll make you do push-ups when you wake up."

"Stop with the coach bullshit. I won't be able to sleep knowing you're curled up like a cannonball on that couch."

"Lily, I'm fine. Seriously. Don't worry about me." I flip to my back and let my legs hang over the armrest."

"Oh my God," Lily exclaims. "No. You're not sleeping like that. In fact, you're getting in bed with me."

Shock vibrates through me, and heat rushes into my gut. Damn her for tempting me like this. I swallow hard, trying to regain control. "No," I say firmly. "That's not a good idea."

"Uh-oh. Is the big guy scared?"

I smile, a bit of the tension releasing from my shoulders. Somehow, she's always able to lighten me up, even when I'm wound tighter than a spring.

Would it really be so bad to share a bed with her? I do need sleep. For all I know, my sleeplessness last night might have contributed to my abysmal performance on the field tonight. Coach won't be happy with me if I slack off tomorrow at practice. Besides, I would never cross a line. Lily trusts me, and I won't betray that trust. It's just a bed, just a few hours of sleep. Nothing more.

"Ethan," Lily drawls my name. "Am I so irresistible that you're afraid you won't be able to keep your hands off me?"

Her taunt snaps me into action. I leap off the couch and stride over to the bed. "Alright, fine. But no funny business, Greenwood."

She giggles. "Funny business. Oh my God, Ethan. You're fucking adorable."

Adorable. I don't think she's ever called me that before, but how many times have I thought it about her? Warmth spreads through me.

The instant I'm under the blankets, the warm feeling builds into a searing heat. Her scent—something floral and uniquely Lily—immediately envelops me, rushing through my senses. I'm not even touching her, but the heat of her body radiates toward me.

Oh, no.

This was a mistake.

I clench my jaw, trying to ignore the rush of sensations. The bed is too small, the air too thick. I lie stiffly on my back, staring at the ceiling, every muscle in my body tensed as if ready to spring away.

"Are you happy now?" I ask, striving for lightness.

She giggles again, the sound sweet and musical. "I can't believe that actually worked."

"Of course it worked. You pulled the age-old tactic of asking if I'm scared. I had to prove I'm a man. Obviously."

"A big, strong man." Her soft hand settles on my arm, and my whole body grows as tight as a clenched fist.

"Lily, please don't do that."

"What?" She sounds genuinely confused.

I try to keep my voice gentle. "Please don't touch me."

She jerks her hand back, and shame fills my gut. It's not her fault that she's tempting me, and I embarrassed her.

"I know you were only teasing, but you have to understand…"

She swallows. "What?"

I can feel her eyes on me, but I don't dare look at her. Instead, I focus on the faint glow from the streetlights filtering through the curtains.

"You're a beautiful girl, and your touch is… It's too much. Do you understand?"

She's quiet for a long while, and I try to retreat into my head to escape my growing anxiety.

"I do," she eventually says, and a jolt rushes through me.

Is she hinting that she wants me too? God, help me. If she does, I don't know how I'll resist her.

Chapter Sixteen

L ily

I'm surrounded by warmth. Strong arms are wrapped around my body, and a steady heartbeat thumps against my back. As I nuzzle deeper, the soft rhythm of breathing lulls me back into the darkness.

I jerk awake, gasping as the realization dawns. It's not just blankets tangled around me, but Ethan's arms too.

That's right. I goaded him into sharing this bed, and now we're cuddling.

And that's not all.

Something big and hard is pressing against my lower back. Heat pools in my belly. For one irrational moment, I relax against his chest and revel in his warmth.

I need to pull away. Ethan already told me that my touch is too much. His principles are strict—the lines of right and wrong drawn firmly in the sand. I don't want to betray him by enjoying the warmth of his body when he doesn't even know what he's doing.

As gently as I can, I try to wriggle out of his arms. I freeze when he stirs and mumbles something incoherent. A moment later, he draws me back against his chest, his grip firm and unyielding. His deep inhale tugs at my hair, as if he's savoring my scent.

I'm startled when his hand drifts downward and creeps around my hips. His rough fingers slip underneath my pajama shirt, settling on my belly. Fingers spread wide, pressing me closer still.

Oh fuck. His touch feels damn good. Pressure builds in my tummy, sending electricity into my thighs.

His lips graze my head, and he hums.

I swallow hard. The one thing I want to do right now is slip my fingers into my panties and ease this unbearable ache.

Instead, I lie as stiff as a board for what feels like an eternity. Eventually, the tension starts to seep out of my body as the rhythmic cadence of his breathing lulls my racing thoughts. A soothing wave of calm settles over me.

I'm safe here in his arms.

A moment later, I'm floating, untethered and serene, as I drift back into the darkness.

* * *

"Get up, Lily. I already gave you an extra ten minutes. I have to go do my workout now."

I groan, the sound muffled by my pillow. He *gave me* ten extra minutes? I don't even remember waking up. My head is fuzzy and quiet. The desire for more sleep is like a boulder in my head, pulling me down, down...

"Up! You can't sleep more than eight hours. We're training your body to sleep at a certain time."

"Got it. Five more minutes."

His rumble of laughter warms me. "Okay, I'll let you cheat this morning, but that's it. I'll give you until I get back from my workout. Forty-five minutes. Deal?"

"Deal," I mumble, my mind already drifting back into the dark haze.

In what feels like seconds later, Ethan's voice pierces into my skull. "Alright, sleepy girl. No more excuses. If you're not up in thirty seconds, I'm pouring cold water on your face."

I whimper. "There's no way that was forty-five minutes. You're a liar."

"That's no way to talk to your coach."

There's a rustle at my feet, and a moment later, the heavy blanket is gone, and cold air hits my skin. "You asshole!"

With monumental effort, I pry my eyes open and push myself into a sitting position. The room swims into focus, revealing Ethan by the kitchenette. God, he looks like a giant next to that tiny counter.

The memory of last night hits me suddenly—the warmth of his body and those rough fingers slipping under my shirt.

Goddamn. He probably doesn't even remember.

And I won't be able to forget.

He grabs a cup from the small cupboard, his movements smooth and sure. His hair is damp, the normally sandy-brown strands looking almost black. He pours some white powder into a glass of water.

"What are you making?" I ask.

"Protein shake."

My nose wrinkles. "That's not what I would call a shake. Why don't you blend some fruit with it?"

He shrugs. "Too much work. I'm used to the taste now."

He stirs a spoon in the glass until the powder dissolves into a cloudy mixture, and I want to gag as he gulps it down.

Gross. I can't watch this any longer.

I push myself off the bed and walk to the duffel bag in the corner of Ethan's room. After pulling out a pair of jeans and a tank top, I glance back at Ethan. He's gulping down the last clump of powder at the bottom of the glass. Bile rises at the back of my throat. "Ethan, oh my God. Why would you drink something so disgusting?"

He stares at me for a long moment, as if considering his answer. He sets the glass down on the counter with a clunk and then grabs the hem of his shirt. In one fluid motion, he peels his shirt over his head and drops it to the floor. His torso is a canvas of ripples and grooves.

Good God. He has muscles I never even knew existed, like those ridges on his shoulders. I love a man's shoulders. They're an underrated body part. Ethan's are so big and wide, like a warrior's.

Liquid warmth rushes into my belly, and my cheeks grow warm. Distantly, I register the smirk on his face as I stand here gawking at him. I need to say something snarky. That's what he would expect.

I can't. My brain is mush.

I think he might be the most beautiful thing I've ever seen.

"That's why," Ethan says with a smirk. He retrieves his shirt from the floor and slips it back over his head.

His cockiness knocks me out of my daze.

When his gaze returns to mine, I pout. "Ethan, I'm so sorry."

His frown is questioning, and I want to draw out his suspense. I saunter over to the counter and lean my hip against it. He stares at me, his expression growing baffled. I set my hand on his muscular arm. "I had no idea you were craving my attention. I've neglected you, huh? It's been over twenty-four hours since I last told you how handsome you are. Just ask me next time you're feeling insecure. I'm here for you, big guy."

His eyelids flutter, though his lips are quirking. "And here I thought I could embarrass you for a change. What the hell was I thinking?"

I giggle. "I don't know. You should know by now that I'm unembarrassable."

He lifts his hand and pokes my nose with his finger. "My sassy girl."

My heart skips a beat. I guess that's his new nickname for me. "Sassy girl," I say softly. "That's kind of cute."

"Yeah?" His voice is raspy. Those dark eyes grow hooded, and he bites his bottom lip. He takes a step forward, closing the space between us. The room seems to shrink, and the air thickens.

My breath catches in my throat. His hand moves slowly, hesitantly, to brush a stray lock of hair behind my ear. The little touch sends a shiver down my spine. His face inches closer, and his breath brushes over my skin.

He pulls back suddenly, shattering the moment.

Goddamn him.

Just kiss me you obsessive, infuriating control freak.

After clearing his throat, his gaze returns to mine. "So I wanted to ask you something..."

I frown. "What?"

"Last night, when we were in bed together..." He scratches the back of his head, his cheeks darkening. "I feel like I might have... I had a dream that I was..."

A wicked thrill courses through me. So he does remember holding me last night, if only vaguely.

And I'm going to punish him for teasing me with that near kiss.

"What?" I ask innocently.

He shuts his eyes and lets out a heavy sigh. "I think I might have...cuddled with you."

I wince. "Oh no, Ethan. Do you really think so? Cuddling..." I shake my head. "That's really bad. A terrible sin, I think. Do you need to call your brother and have him...pour some holy water on you or something?"

His expression grows so comically exasperated that I burst

into laughter. It echoes through the room, and Ethan only stands there rolling his eyes.

"Holy water," he scoffs. "You know nothing about protestant Christianity. No, I wasn't bringing it up because of my religion, but because of you."

I wave a hand. "Why would a wild girl like me stress about a little cuddling?"

His frown is incredulous. "I meant because of...Mason. He assaulted you. I thought maybe you wouldn't...want to be touched by a guy after that."

Holy shit.

An ethereal sensation wraps around me, making the world around me buzz and blur. I just spent the night in bed with a man. Not only that, but he wrapped his arms around me and held me tightly when I tried to move away.

But my body wasn't afraid. I didn't even think about Mason once.

Because I was lying in Ethan's arms, and Ethan isn't Mason. The two are as different as bubblegum and thunderclouds.

Ethan is safe.

I swallow. "Last night was different. I trust you."

His eyes widen minutely. He stares at me for a long moment, as if trying to puzzle out my words. Then the corners of his mouth lift, and a slow, radiant smile breaks across his face. "I'm glad." His voice is breathless.

My cheeks warm at his sudden intensity. Shouldn't it be a given that I trust him? He's the most principled person I know.

"When is your first class?" he asks.

I frown. "At noon. Why?"

He grins. "Mine is at one. Why don't we head to campus together and grab an early lunch?"

My tummy flips over. It feels like he's asking me on a date, even though I know that's not the case.

But I wouldn't mind if he did. It's time to finally admit to myself why I've been drawn to Ethan Harrington all these years, even when I told myself he drove me nuts.

It was a crush. One that I tried to suppress because Lily Greenwood doesn't chase after guys who don't like her back.

After getting to know him better, it's become so much more than a crush.

I trust this man. I know in my soul he would upend the whole world to shield me from harm. Because he has integrity.

It's a quality I underrated until that night with Mason.

Chapter Seventeen

E^{than}

She trusts me. My God, she trusts me. Enough to let me cuddle with her during the night without pulling away.

The thought alone is like a drug pumping through my veins. It's even more potent than the pleasure of waking up with her soft body in my arms last night, for the brief moment I indulged in it before pulling away.

Should I be this exhilarated? Gaining her trust was supposed to be for her sake, not mine. I was called by God to help her because she's in a dark place. Mason hurt her. I know he did. I need her to open up to me so that I can help her take action. To protect herself from being hurt by him in the future.

But her trust feels like so much more somehow. Like the beginning of something bright and beautiful.

When I glance over at Lily, she's nibbling on her burrito, looking lost in thought. I lean back onto the lawn, letting the afternoon sunlight warm my face. The breeze toys with her fiery-red hair that seems almost too intense to be real, too vivid.

Just like her.

"Is that your natural hair color?" I ask.

Lily raises an eyebrow, a playful smirk tugging on her lips. "Is that a roundabout way of asking me if the carpets match the drapes?"

I grimace, though my gut clenches. "Gross. I'd never ask a question like that, which you well know."

It *is* a gross question, but the image that floods into my mind isn't. I see her sitting with her legs spread. I'll bet she has a beautiful pussy—pink and glistening...

I have to stop thinking this way. I'm going to lose my mind.

Lily twists a lock of her hair around her finger. "I'm actually more of a reddish-blond naturally. But I started dyeing it bright red in high school. I think it fits my personality."

I chuckle. "You're right about that. You're a firecracker."

"Do you like that I'm a firecracker, Ethan?"

"You know I do." The words flow out of my mouth, as if they have a will of their own.

Our eyes lock, and my heart thumps against my chest. This is a dangerous conversation, teasing words to my lips that I can never utter.

You make it seem worth it to throw my whole religion away and worship you instead.

God, forgive me for that wicked thought.

"I just remembered something," Lily says. "You should know that the carpets don't match the drapes because you've seen me naked before. Remember? I took all my clothes off at that beer pong tournament."

Heat suffuses my skin. As if I'd ever forget. Except I don't have a clear image of her body. I forced myself to keep my eyes fixed on her face when I scolded her.

I regretted that when I reflected back on it later. In fact, I've called that fuzzy image of her bare, delicate curves to mind, straining to remember every blurred detail.

That should have been a sign that my body was secretly burning for her, but I've been in deep denial.

Lily giggles. "You were ready to kill me. I don't think I've ever seen you so pissed off."

"I *was* pissed off. You put me in a really awkward position. No one wants to be caught staring at his best friend's sister's naked body."

Or being caught in a jealous rage because of all the other guys staring at her naked body.

Her bright-gray eyes grow huge. "You were staring at me?"

My pulse speeds up. How much should I tell her? I suppose only the truth.

"I forced myself not to look, but it was difficult."

Her smile is a little naughty. Fuck, she's so cute.

"It was?" she asks.

I snort. "Of course. You're a beautiful girl."

"I wanted you to see me," she says with a hint of defiance. "I'm pretty sure I fell in the toilet just to piss you off."

I grin, shaking my head. That night, she told everyone she fell in the toilet and got so wet she had to take off all her clothes. I knew it was a lie. Lily loves to cause trouble.

But I had no idea it was for me. Even if it was only to tease me, I don't care. She's revealing something about herself whether she knows it or not.

We're both drawn to each other. There's an undeniable pull between us, an electric current that ignites whenever we're together. Our personalities clash and blend in ways that feel almost...inevitable.

Lily's head jerks up as she stares over my shoulder. Her face grows white and taut, and the hairs on my arms stand up.

"So the two of you are a couple now?" a grating voice asks from behind me.

When I twist around, there stands Mason. His eyes are

narrowed, and his jaw is clenched so tightly it looks like it might crack.

I'm on my feet in an instant. "Do you have a death wish?" I hover over him, mimicking his aggressive posture. "Don't you ever come near her again."

"Death wish," Mason mutters, his gaze scanning my face. "What did she tell you?" His head jerks in Lily's direction. "If I find out..." His mouth tightens, his whole body vibrating with tension. "You'd better keep your mouth shut, Lily. I told you my family has a lawyer."

My head grows fuzzy. "Lawyer?" I murmur.

What the hell is he talking about? I already know that he grabbed her by the wrists. I saw him do it. Why is he worried that she told me something?

He must be talking about something else. Something much worse than grabbing her wrists.

A thought comes to mind, something so ugly I want to push it away. Lily's been acting differently these past several months. Withdrawn. Anxious. Unable to focus. Aren't those signs of someone who was...

Oh, fuck.

My face drains of heat, and time seems to slow. When I glance at Lily, my focus narrows, like I'm on the field. Every tiny movement is somehow bigger. Her hands are shaking, and the pulse at her neck is flickering madly.

My God, she's terrified of him.

I inhale a shaky breath. "If you don't leave right the fuck now, I will break your nose, my football career be damned."

He must sense the seriousness in my words, because he backs up several steps. "Lily," he calls out. "You'd better not have told him anything. I promise it won't end well for you."

Lily scoffs, but I can see that it took effort. Her lips are trembling. "You're calling yourself out, Mason, not me. And I don't think you understand how lawyers work."

Mason scowls. "You can go to jail for slander."

Lily's smile doesn't reach her eyes. "No, you can't, dumbass. Slander is a civil offense. A single Google search could have told you that."

Mason's face grows hesitant for the first time. "You can't... There's no way you can prove anything happened."

"Get the fuck out of here," Lily says, her voice shaking. "Just looking at you is ruining my appetite." She drops her burrito onto the paper plate in front of her.

Mason hesitates and then turns on his heel and walks away with stiff, angry strides.

My heart races, panic vibrating through my entire body. "What the hell was that about?"

My eyes scan her face for clues, for anything that might unravel the knot in my stomach.

Lily's lips tremble, and she bites down hard. A single tear escapes, rolling down her cheek. She quickly wipes it away, but more follow, and her shoulders start to shake.

Slowly, she crumbles, burying her face in her hands as silent sobs wrack her body. A knife twists deep into my heart. The sight of her crying is an agony I've never known.

Oh God, he really hurt her. He hurt her, and I'm going to make him pay.

And if that's not enough to keep her safe, I'll sell my soul to the fucking devil.

Chapter Eighteen

L ily

I'm pulled against a hard chest, held so tightly that breathing becomes a struggle. Yet the sobs come anyway, relentless and unstoppable. They crash over me like waves against the shore. Inevitable. It's as though by holding them back, I've been defying the natural order of things.

A heavy sense of relief settles over me as the tears flow freely, so profound that it's almost dizzying. The weight that has been pressing down on my chest for so long has finally given way.

The world around me is sharper, more vivid, and at least in this moment, I'm the old Lily.

I'm so grateful for this man who holds me in his arms and lets me cry without judgment. He hasn't spoken since that first tear fell, like my crying is the most normal thing in the world. He doesn't even know what Mason did.

His steadiness and integrity—qualities I once dismissed as boring—fill me with an overwhelming sense of safety. In his presence, I have no fear, which allows me to confront the shadows of my past.

Is this wrong? I shouldn't need him to cope with my trauma. The only person I should need is myself.

Oh well. For now, I'll take his comfort.

"Lily." Ethan's voice shakes.

I twist my head to rest my cheek against his chest. His shirt is now damp from my tears. "Thank you," I whisper.

His warm lips brush against my head. "I won't push you to talk, but...not knowing what Mason did is making me crazy."

When I look up at him, his face is strained, the muscles taut. The pain in his eyes is so palpable I could reach out and touch it.

He's holding it all in, just for me, and it sends a pang to my chest.

"I'm here for you," he says, his voice thick, "whether you want to tell me or not. But watching you in pain, seeing you go through this alone..." His lips quiver. "It's killing me."

"I want to tell you," I say, surprised by my own admission. "I think I'm ready. I never... For some reason, I didn't want to tell anyone until now."

It's strange now that I think about it. What was I so afraid of?

I never really knew. I was just running. Running so fast I never had the chance to look deep inside and learn my own heart.

He tightens his hold on me, his fingers tracing circles on my back. "Then tell me. Let me share this burden with you."

My heart grows quiet, and a deep, comforting warmth settles over my body.

I could fall in love with this man if I allow myself.

Even though I embrace my own chaos, I'm also hungry for his dependability. He's like a missing piece in my heart, the one I didn't even know I was searching for.

"I can't tell you now," I say. "My class is in twenty minutes."

"Fuck class. We're both skipping. This is too big of a deal. We're going home."

Home. I love the word on his lips. As if that bedroom we've

shared for the past few days is ours alone. A haven, just for the two of us.

This deep connection between us may only be temporary—it may only last while I'm staying at his place—but I'll take it. Somehow, I don't feel weak accepting his help.

Maybe it's okay to need other people, to lean on them when the burden becomes too heavy to bear alone. After crying in Ethan's arms, I'm finally able to breathe again. It's not just about surviving anymore. Maybe I can finally start living again.

* * *

I'm nestled in the corner of the couch as Ethan moves around the table at the edge of his room. The electric kettle clicks on, and its soft hum fills the silence between us.

"Who'd you steal the kettle from?"

His face is grim. Poor guy has been vibrating with tension since our walk home from campus.

"I bought it last night," he says. "For your chamomile tea. The old one in our kitchen is grimy and nasty."

This man is so thoughtful. How is it that just weeks ago I still thought he was a high-handed prick who judges me for my messiness?

Ethan's movements are jerky as he steeps the teabag, which is at odds with his athletic grace. I can't help but smile.

"Let me do that. You're anxious, big guy. I guess I can't blame you after my crying fit."

He frowns as he hands me the teacup. "I wish you didn't minimize what you're going through. And don't worry about me, damn it. I'll be just fine. I'm worried about you."

His words make my chest grow tight. When tears start welling behind my eyes, I take a deep breath through my nose.

No more crying. It's time to confront reality head-on, to embrace the emotions I've long suppressed.

I take a sip of the tea, the taste somehow bland and bitter at the same time. "Ethan, I don't even like chamomile tea. This isn't bedtime, so I'm not sure why you made it for me."

He sits down on the couch beside me, his expression growing grave. "I'm sorry. When I'm feeling this...wound up, I have to take action, and I guess I was trying to help you relax. I'm losing my mind right now. Are you ready to talk to me?

My chest squeezes tightly. I don't want him to be so anxious. It's difficult to see.

"Yes," I say.

Time for the truth, no matter how little I want to face it.

I can do this. If crying was a relief, telling the whole ugly story might be too.

When I open my lips, a wave of cold, sick shame washes over me suddenly. Where does this feeling come from? It's completely irrational. It wasn't my fault that Mason raped me.

"About six months ago," I say. "Mason and I were out at the bars. I was on the verge of breaking up with him. He was becoming sort of...pushy. He wanted things his way, especially when it came to..." I swallow. "Sex."

Ethan shuts his eyes tightly, looking so anguished I want to reach out and touch him.

It's going to be hard for him to hear the ugly details—as protective as he is of me—but I can't think about that.

What happened to me *was* ugly, and I had to live through it. His discomfort in hearing it is nothing compared to what I endured. I deserve to speak my truth.

"Anyway." I tug at a loose thread on the seam of my jeans. "I let him walk me home, even though I was over his shit. When we got to my sorority house, he wanted to come inside. He was insistent on it, acting like I owed it to him after he walked me home."

Ethan grunts. When I lift my gaze to his face, his jaw is clenched. "What a fucking dirtbag."

I smile sadly. Mason's behavior must be incomprehensible to Ethan. In his eyes, walking a girl home at night is simply the right thing to do. But Mason's sense of entitlement isn't unusual. Over the years, I've met many men who believe they deserve access to me for the bare minimum of kindness.

Normally, I'd tell men like that to go to hell. But that night, I was so damn tired and drunk. I just didn't think.

"Anyway, I let him come inside." I shut my eyes when shame wells in my chest. "I even let him sleep in my bed. But I did make it clear that I didn't want to be touched."

"But he touched you anyway." Ethan's words are delivered through clenched teeth.

"Yes." My voice is just above a whisper. "Within seconds of getting into bed, he was on top of me, grinding into me and pulling up my dress. I kept telling him to stop." My throat is so strained that it's difficult to get the words out. "He didn't."

Ethan leaps off the couch and starts pacing the floor, his hands clenching into fists. "Oh fuck, Lily." He shakes his head, looking dazed. "I'm going to make him pay."

He means it. I can hear it in his voice, and though his strong reaction is somewhat soothing, it doesn't stop irritation from flaring over my skin.

"No, big guy." I try to keep my voice soft. "I know you're upset, but you can't make this about you. It's my place to make Mason pay, and I've already done my research. Rape is really hard to prove if you were already in a sexual relationship with the person. It's basically your word against theirs."

Twin strips of pink burnish Ethan's cheeks. "Maybe, but using the law isn't the only way to make sure he faces consequences. Mason cares about football more than anything. I know if Coach Rodriguez heard this, Mason would be off the team."

"I can't believe you of all people would suggest that. Noah told me you'll get drafted if you finish this season strong. I don't know much about football, but even my ignorant ass knows a quarterback is important."

He scowls. "It makes me crazy that you think I'd put my football career over you. Mason can't get away with what he did. Who gives a fuck about football?"

The idea that Ethan would put me before his football career, a future he's worked so hard for, makes my heart squeeze in my chest. But then again, it's probably just his principles guiding him. His devotion to do what's right at all costs.

"You know Mason would deny it," I say. "Loudly, too. He'd blast me on social media. And he's well-known on campus. If I got him kicked off the team, I'd probably be harassed by all the misogynistic gym rats who worship the Hawks."

Ethan stands up, crossing his arms over his chest. "He's not as well-known as I am. Or as well-liked."

I frown. "So?"

"So you'd have my full support. I'll even go on social media to call him out, and I have my own eyes to back me up." His jaw clenches. "I saw him grab you."

There's a buzzing sound in my ears. He suggested this once before, but I didn't take him seriously. But that was before I was willing to confront my pain. I wanted to ignore it, pretend it wasn't there.

Should I come forward? I've barely considered it until now, but everything Ethan has said is reasonable. He's the star of the whole school. It wouldn't be my word over Mason's, but mine and Ethan's.

It would be exhilarating to make that bastard suffer for what he so readily dismissed months ago and has continued to taunt me about. I'd love to see his downfall, but then again...

Everyone on campus would know about what happened to me. It would become a label branded to my forehead—the girl who was raped. With Ethan's national attention, the whole incident could become a public scandal. It might even follow me for the rest of my life.

I can't allow that. I'm not the girl who was raped. I'm Lily Greenwood, the girl who was once fun and carefree, and I'm going to reclaim her. No matter what it takes.

"No," I say firmly.

Ethan's eyes shut, and he drops his head forward. "Lily."

My nostrils flare. "Don't 'Lily' me. I've already been through enough. Shouldn't I be able to deal with this on my own terms?" I run my fingers through my hair and grip hard, sending tingles into my scalp. "I hate everything about what happened. I want it all to go away."

When Ethan opens his eyes, they're full of pain. "I don't think it works like that. I think..." He inhales a shaky breath. "I hate even saying this, but I think this might always be a part of you."

An icy hand clamps around my heart. No, I won't allow that. I've heard the clichés about trauma becoming a part of who you are.

This pain—this fear—it won't claim me.

"But it doesn't mean you'll always be traumatized by it," Ethan says. "In some ways, it'll make you more resilient."

Resilient. What an Ethan word to use. As if everything in life is just an opportunity for self-improvement. As if pain and fear can simply be repurposed into another step toward some ideal version of myself.

This is how perfectionists cope. They have to turn every wound into a lesson, to believe that suffering can be transformed into strength. Otherwise, it's just suffering.

I take no comfort in lessons, in building strength. What does any of it matter if there's no joy?

"Lily..." Ethan's rough voice pulls me out of my head. "I need to tell you something. It's something I think you already know, but I'm afraid... I can't end this conversation without telling you on the off chance that some part of you hasn't accepted it."

I frown. "What?"

He slips down to his knees in front of me, taking both my hands in his. His eyes burn into mine. "No part of what happened was your fault. Not dating Mason in the first place or letting him come inside that night. Not getting into bed with him or being too small to fight him off. None of it."

His words wash over me like a tropical rain, and the vestiges of shame and regret fall away.

In theory, I knew that none of it was my fault, but I couldn't fight the nagging fear and regret of being an accomplice in my own assault. If only I hadn't been so drunk... If only I hadn't let him come inside...

Ethan is right. No part of what Mason did is my fault. Getting too drunk wasn't a request to be raped.

Tears prick my eyes. "Thank you."

Ethan gathers me into his arms and pulls me onto his lap. His warmth seeps into all my cold places. We sit this way for who knows how long. Time seems to slow.

"I want to take you out tonight," he says a while later, his arms still wrapped around me. "We'll go when I get back from practice. Anywhere you want."

A dreamy smile spreads across my face. "Sounds wonderful."

Chapter Nineteen

L ily

As we stand in line for the club, Ethan's hand rests on my lower back, sending a delicious heat into my belly.

My spirit has been as light as air all day, and I think it's because confessing to Ethan released a smothering weight on my chest. One I carried for six months.

I might finally be on the path toward finding my old self, and tonight, I'm testing it.

Clubs and parties lost their appeal after my drunken night with Mason, but I miss being out in large groups of people. I asked Ethan to take me to some of my old favorite spots downtown so we can drink and dance and reclaim my former life.

Our first stop was at one of my favorite bars, and I begged Ethan to take shots with me. I haven't drunk at all in six months —alcohol was too closely tied to the night my life unraveled. Tonight is different.

I'm with Ethan. Ethan is safe.

And he's completely adorable when he's drunk.

He transformed after those shots. I could see all over his face the moment the alcohol finally hit. His gaze softened, and a subtle, inviting smile played at the corners of his lips. He started touching me constantly. Not anywhere interesting—unfortunately—but even his innocent touches give me a delicious thrill.

"Are you cold?" Ethan's warm breath tickles my ear. He sets both hands on my shoulders, his thumb caressing my back.

A giggle escapes my lips. "Ethan, you're so drunk."

"No way. I'm only buzzed."

When I twist around and see his face, I laugh harder. His grin is silly and almost boyish. This is a piece of him I've never seen in all these years. I've seen him at parties, but he's never had more than one beer.

He's letting go tonight. For me.

"*I'm* drunk?" Ethan says. "You're laughing about nothing."

"You wouldn't think it was nothing if you could see your face."

I'm startled when he lifts his hand high in the air and brings it down on my ass with a resounding smack. My stomach fills with heat even as my mouth drops open in shock. "What has gotten into you?"

His expression grows puzzled. "I don't know. I just wanted to do it. I think I am drunk."

My own buzz makes me bold. I step forward and lift my chin, and his warm, slightly boozy breath brushes over my face. "It would be a lot more fun over your lap."

His eyes grow molten as they lock on my face. The air between us seems to crackle. He takes a step, closing the already minimal space between us. The heat of his body radiates toward me.

"Move!" A voice says from behind us.

It's probably a good thing. I don't want him telling me tomorrow that he only broke his vow never to kiss me again because he was drunk.

It'll make my hangover even worse.

Ethan doesn't seem to notice that we're holding up the line. His hungry gaze is still fixed on my mouth. I grab his hand and pull him forward to move with the line. The bass from within the club pulses like a second heartbeat under our feet, and when we finally make it inside, we're enveloped by a kaleidoscope of lights and the thumping music.

I missed this club. It's so delightfully trashy.

"Alright, big guy," I shout over the music. "The first thing we're doing is getting water."

"Hell, no," he shouts back. "We're dancing first."

Ethan pulls me out onto the dance floor, his eyes shimmering with energy.

Once we're swallowed into the crowd, Ethan yanks my body against his. His hips move fluidly with the music, and bafflement expands within me like a rising tide. Who would have thought uptight Ethan Harrington would be such a good dancer? This man knows how to move.

"You're a hella good dancer," I shout. "How did that happen?"

He grins, pulling me closer. "I'm an athlete. I'm good at anything that involves my body."

Heat stirs in my gut. I'm not sure if he meant the sexual innuendo, but it certainly seems like it based on his wicked smile.

The thing is, I think Ethan would be good at sex, even on his first try. His ability to move his body is only part of it. He also has that razor-sharp focus and determination. He wouldn't rest until he made me come.

A molten heat rushes through my veins. Damn his stupid chastity pledge.

"You're a better dancer than me, big guy," I say.

When he lets out a groan, I frown. "What?"

His hand slides up to cradle my face, and his thumb brushes my cheekbone. "I love it when you call me 'big guy.'"

Under the pulsing lights, Ethan's eyes hold mine with an

intensity that makes heat coil in my belly, ready to burst. With each beat, he draws me closer until we're barely a breath apart.

It's too much. I need some space from him or I might make the drunken decision to close the distance between us and press my lips against his.

I clear my throat. "You know...there's a pole in this club."

"A what?"

"A pole," I shout, my ears starting to ring from the blasting music. "For dancing. My sorority sisters and I love this club because it's such a dive for Santa Barbara." An idea sprouts, making my stomach flip over. "Oh my God! What if we had a pole dancing competition?"

His appalled expression makes me giggle. Damn, I must be more drunk than I thought, challenging Ethan of all people to a pole dance off.

I cock a brow. "What? Are you scared?"

He snorts and shakes his head. "What does pole dancing competition even mean? How would we decide the winner? I'm very competitive, sassy girl. We need to have rules."

I cross my arms over my chest. "What do you take me for, a pole dancing virgin? My sorority sisters and I have done this plenty of times. We judge the performance based on how many cheers we get."

He scowls. "Naturally, you'll win that. You're fucking gorgeous."

My belly warms as it always does when Ethan compliments my appearance. "You're not exactly ugly. Plus, you're famous. I'm actually at a huge disadvantage here. In fact, I'll make you go first to warm up the crowd for me. You'll take a handicap to make it fair."

Ethan's fingers drum against his thigh as he glances around the dance floor, clearly conflicted. He finally sighs and runs a hand through his hair. "Alright, fine. But if a YouTube video of me dancing on that pole goes viral and ends up on some sports news segment, I'll give you that spanking over my lap."

My breath hitches, a jolt of excitement mingling with nerves. "Deal."

He grabs my hand and starts pulling me through the crowd, marching in the direction of the pole on the corner stage. He's so big and tall that people seem to step out of his way instinctively, creating a clear path for us.

We're lucky that the tiny stage is empty when we make it to the corner of the club. Ethan leaps up onto it and grips the pole. He glances back at me, his eyes glinting with challenge and amusement.

"Go, Ethan!" I shout. "Show them what you've got!"

His eyes are locked on mine as he starts dancing. He takes on a mock seductive look, placing one finger on his full lips. He moves around the pole with exaggerated hip swings and body rolls, making me laugh so hard that tears spring to my eyes.

"Is that Ethan Harrington?" someone behind me asks.

I turn around to see what looks like a college guy with tousled brown hair. "Yep," I say. "He's considering pole dancing as a career if he doesn't get drafted."

This guy must not be the only one who noticed Ethan on stage, because the erupting cheers around me are almost deafening.

The guy grins as his gaze shifts to the stage. "I think he might want to stick to football."

"What are you talking about?" I gesture at Ethan. "He's an expert dancer. Look at those hip thrusts."

The guy moves closer to me, his breath brushing against my ear. "I'd like to see you up there."

I roll my eyes and take a step forward. Ethan seems to notice our exchange, because his playful expression is gone, and his gaze is fixed on the guy behind me. His final dance move is a dramatic spin around the pole. He leaps off the stage and wraps his arm around my waist, yanking me against his hard chest. He shoots a dirty look over his shoulder that I have to assume is for the guy who flirted with me.

My tummy does a little turn. When did his overprotectiveness become so hot?

His dark-blue eyes are hooded. "Was that guy bothering you?"

"Not enough to ruin my enjoyment of your truly innovative performance. Did you end it just because of him?"

"Maybe." Ethan's lips twist into a half smile. "Or maybe I just wanted an excuse to touch you."

A flutter of excitement dances in my chest. I shoot him a cheeky smile. "It was a mistake. You didn't give the crowd enough time to heat up. You gave me an advantage."

He lifts his hand and strokes a thumb over my cheekbone, sending electricity down my spine. "Let's see what you've got, sassy girl."

He guides me to the pole. When we make it to the steps, he grabs me by the waist and hoists me on the stage. Warmth fills my belly. He really is using any excuse to touch me.

I fucking love it.

Chapter Twenty

E^{than}

Lily spins around the pole, her energy infectious. With a cocked brow, she blows kisses in my direction.

Fuck, I love her playfulness. I wish I could capture her sparkle like fireflies in a mason jar.

My body is as light as it's been in years, and it isn't because of the alcohol. Somehow, Lily has the power to unlock parts of me I didn't even know were closed off. No one else in the world could have coaxed me up onto the stage, let alone make me feel so at ease while doing something as ridiculous as pole dancing in public.

Here I am, entranced by her vivacity, loving every second of it.

Noah would think I've lost my mind, taking his little sister out to get drunk and accepting her challenge to a pole dancing competition. He'd probably be more baffled than angry, thinking he never really knew me. The thought of breaking his trust should fill me with sick dread.

It doesn't. Somehow, tonight, there's only Lily and the strange quiet that settles in my heart whenever she's around.

Lily arches her back, surprising me with a move that has her spinning upside down, her hair cascading toward the floor like a waterfall. Laughter lights her eyes, but there's a sultry grace to her now, a deliberate teasing in the way she looks over at me before flipping upright once more.

Heat coils in my stomach, tight and urgent. I want this woman. In this moment, I want her so badly I could grab her from that stage and rush her back to my house, breaking my vow to save myself for my future wife.

It's probably the alcohol thinking for me. I can't allow myself to drink any more, or I'll lose my head entirely.

The crowd erupts around me, drawing my attention to the guy making his way toward the stage. It's the dude from earlier who was hovering over Lily and whispering into her ear. He walks up the steps and grabs the pole.

Oh. Fuck. No.

A dark surge of protectiveness takes hold of me, twisting my gut and making my hands clench into fists.

Lily's eyes flash with a hint of annoyance as she spins away from him. She twists her hips and ducks under his outstretched arm. She's not amused.

My feet pull me forward as if they have a will of their own. When I make it to the stage, I clamp my hand around the metal pole, using it to vault myself up beside them. Lily's eyes meet mine, wide with surprise.

With effort, I smile lazily at the guy. "I hope you don't mind if I steal my girlfriend back."

He frowns in what looks like disbelief and maybe a hint of anxiety.

With that, I grab Lily's waist and lift her into my arms. The crowd roars again, this time mixed with gasps and whispers.

Lily's weight is nothing as I jump off the stage. Her arms

drape over my shoulders. "Cheater!" she shouts. "You only did that because you wanted me to lose our—"

I crash my mouth against hers to silence her. For a moment, the world fades away, and there's nothing but the softness of her lips pressed against mine.

Fuck, I want to take her home. I want to crawl into that bed with her and assuage this unbearable ache inside.

It takes all my willpower to pull back and break the kiss. Her eyebrows shoot up. She bites her bottom lip, her cheeks turning a delightful shade of pink. "You kissed me."

I smile. "I did.

She stares at me for a long moment. "I thought you... You said you were never going to do it again."

My whole body grows tense. Holy shit. I vowed I would never kiss her again, and I just did it on a whim.

Why the fuck don't I feel bad about it? If Noah were here, he would kill me, and I don't even care.

I'm changing. Becoming someone I don't know.

My sole connection to God has been a strong inner sense of right and wrong. If I don't have that, what does my faith even mean?

"I like it when you kiss me, Ethan. I wish you'd never made that promise."

My gaze snaps to her face, my pulse pounding against my throat. "Really?"

When she nods, an overwhelming warmth washes over me. I'm never as light and easy and joyful as when I'm with her. Would it be so bad to sin a little for a single night? I won't go any further than kisses, and I can go back to my normal, principled self tomorrow when I'm sober.

I lift my hand and brush my thumb over her full bottom lip. "If you're okay with it, I am too. You were the one who told me promises to ourselves don't matter."

She smiles mischievously. "Especially stupid promises."

I touch the tip of her nose. "Especially those."

A while later, we're sitting at the bar, and I ask the bartender for two waters. When I glance over my shoulder at Lily, her gaze is fixed on her phone. Her brows are knit together, and her mouth is slightly open.

"Everything okay?" I ask.

Her gaze flickers to mine, and something that looks like wariness creeps into her eyes. "Remember Jake?"

"Yep." The word comes out tight, clipped. I lean against the bar and tap my fingers against the wood.

She pauses for a beat, as if considering her words. "He asked me to go out with a group of friends tomorrow night. He wrote me almost an entire novel, telling me he knows it's last minute and his feelings won't be hurt if I say no. I think he was nervous, which is...kind of cute, actually."

A prickling sensation crawls up my spine, and a molten heat surges in my chest. I'm not jealous that she called him cute. That would be stupid.

She already told me she likes him. There's nothing new about this.

"Yeah?" I say tightly.

She's watching me closely now. Am I showing my discomfort?

"Should I say yes?" she asks.

The hairs on my arms stand up. Somehow, I get the feeling that she's calling me out. I kissed her, and I told her I wasn't troubled by it. I hinted I might even do it again. Is she goading me to tell her no, that the thought of her with another man makes me want to hit something?

I don't have the right to tell her no. I've already crossed so many lines tonight. If she likes this guy, she should go out with him. She and I have no future. Even if Noah lets go of his stupid rule, my first girlfriend will be my future wife.

So why am I so conflicted? Lily will probably have a string of boyfriends in the future. If I don't want to be with her, I'll have to get over it. She'll always be a part of my life through Noah, even if

I make it to the NFL and move to a different state when college ends in eight months.

An image flashes in my mind of Lily years from now. She's sitting across from me at a restaurant table with a faceless man by her side and a baby on her lap.

She's laughing. Laughing with that infectious joy that calls to me like the first rays of sunlight after a long, cold night.

Longing grips my chest so tightly that it steals the breath from my lungs.

"Are you okay?" she asks, a crease forming between her brows.

No, I'm not okay. I'm plummeting off a precipice.

I take a deep breath to calm my buzzing thoughts. "If you like him, you should say yes." There's a painful heaviness in my heart as I say the words, but I'll have to live with it. Pain is a part of life. It will make me stronger.

The thought isn't comforting.

"Really?" Her voice is laced with a hint of surprise. Or is it disappointment? "It'll be my first date since...everything happened with Mason."

"Do you trust this guy?" My voice is sharper than I intended.

Lily's gaze holds mine, her eyes deep gray pools of unreadable emotion. Her fingers hover over the screen of her phone. Then she starts tapping rapidly. My heart pounds as she presses the send button with a flick of her thumb.

"I just told him yes," she says. "To answer your question, I don't know him well enough to trust him, but I like his vibe. Plus, we'll be out with other people." Her smile doesn't reach her eyes. "I'm proud of myself. This is a step toward healing, I think."

I try to smile, but my muscles are too tight. I ought to be happy. This is a good step for her.

But fuck, I don't want her going out with another man. I'll be waiting at home, agonizing over what she's doing.

"Good." The word tastes like ash in my mouth. "I'm proud of you, too."

Chapter Twenty-One

E than

"Are you okay?" Noah asks. "You seem distracted."

I fight the urge to wince. I came to this bar after our game to distract myself from Lily, not spend the whole night thinking about her. Noah gets the same beer every time, and I sip my water while we watch footage on my iPad of our next opposing team, analyzing their defensive schemes. It's our ritual.

Not tonight. I didn't even remember to throw my iPad in my gym bag this afternoon.

All I can think about is Lily and her date tonight. My whole body is buzzing with tension.

What if she falls for him?

I'm a fool for even caring. I've made my choice. My vow to my future wife is more important than my seemingly unquenchable thirst for Lily. I couldn't share my bed with her last night when we got home from the clubs. I knew if I did, I would be lost. I'd kiss her again, and that would lead to who knows what.

It ought to alarm me. I've never even considered breaking my purity pledge until now, and I've had millions of opportunities to do so between high school and college.

Where is God? He normally fills my heart with guilt. Even over petty sins like white lies or the feeling of envy. But after calling me to help Lily that day on my jog, he's gone silent.

For the first time in my life, I feel abandoned by him, and it fills me with a simmering anger. It's eerily similar to the day my mom and I came home from an away game to find every trace of my dad's existence wiped from our house.

"I'm fine," I say a touch too quickly. "I'm stressed lately because of... You know...all the pressure of finishing this season strong."

He leans forward, his fingers tapping on the wooden table. "You're killing it, Ethan. You have no reason to— Oh shit." He points a finger over my shoulder. "Speaking of which... There you are on TV."

When I crane my neck, there I am, sprinting across the screen. The ball shoots toward my outstretched hands. I grasp it for a moment before it slips through my fingers and falls with a bounce.

A moment later, an announcer appears on the screen. "It's been tough for this young man," he says. "There were a lot of expectations after his performance against Redwood State last year. You just have to wonder if the pressure of the moment is getting to him."

Noah snorts. "Because of one dropped pass?"

I take a sip of my water. "It was my second of the game. Thank God we won, or else they probably wouldn't be talking about me at all."

It's crazy that I can't even bring myself to care what the commentators say. All I can think about is the night ahead of me.

Waiting for Lily to come home will be agony. What if she doesn't come home at all? One-night stands are common among most college students, and Lily might see safe, consensual sex as a step toward healing. Though she hasn't explicitly said so, I doubt she's had sex with anyone since Mason.

An image flashes in my mind. Her beautiful face flushed and glistening with sweat. Those stormy-gray eyes dark and hooded. A body covers her, grinding into her rounded hips.

Fuck. I have to get out of here. I'm spiraling, and I don't want Noah to see.

Plus, I want to get home before she leaves. I won't contemplate why just yet.

"I gotta head out," I say as I slide out of the booth.

Noah frowns. "Dude, you'd better not be freaking out over what that commentator said. Like you said, they wouldn't be talking about you at all if you hadn't single-handedly turned that game around."

That's not what I said, but I won't correct him. Now that I've made the decision to go home, my heart is thumping so hard it feels like it might burst out of my chest. "It's not that. I just remembered...something I have to do."

Noah's brows knit together. "Um...okay. See you tomorrow."

He's obviously puzzled by my odd, restless behavior, but I can't stay any longer to explain myself. The urgency to leave is pulsing within me.

I have to get home before she leaves for her date.

I jump into my car and race through the streets. Probably a mistake given the fact that getting pulled over by a cop is the last thing I need right now. I can't seem to stop myself. My grip tightens on the steering wheel, and my knuckles turn white.

What am I planning to do, stop her from leaving? Tell her I can't stand the thought of her in the arms of another man? What then?

I haven't answered my own questions by the time I pull up in front of the frat house. After rushing through the front door, I slam it behind me. I force myself to take measured steps up the stairs to my room, but it's difficult. I'd much rather take them two at a time. I take a deep breath before opening the door.

And there she is.

She turns to me, smiling, and my knees start to tremble. Her red hair hangs over her shoulders in soft waves. Her lips are painted in a dark, bold color that contrasts starkly with her fair skin. That burgundy dress clings to her curves, revealing her long, shapely legs.

"You look gorgeous," I croak out.

What an understatement. She's a fucking masterpiece.

She shoots me a cheeky expression before sauntering over to my closet mirror. She sways her hips from side to side as she examines herself. "I'm way overdressed, but I don't care. This is my first date in months, so I'm making it count." She twists around, flipping her hair over her shoulder. "If Jake's mouth doesn't drop open when he sees me, I'll question his taste."

I swallow, inwardly begging my pulse to slow down. "You'll have to send him packing. No sense going on a date with a dumbass."

She tilts her head to the side as she stares at me. Did I say too much? I don't want her to go, damn it, but I thought I made it sound lighthearted and unserious.

"I disagree," she says. "Dummies can be fun, at least in the short-term. You know how I love to have fun."

Jesus, help me. What does she mean by fun? Is she talking about sex?

Anxiety grips my chest, making my vision blur.

She glances at her phone and winces. "I need to head to the front of the sorority house. He's picking me up there since I didn't want... You know, to have him think I live in a frat house."

My smile feels like more of a grimace. "Which you do. In my bedroom."

She narrows her eyes, looking puzzled. Maybe she heard the dark possessiveness in my voice. But if she has a question, she doesn't ask. She walks to the door, and a wave of panic rises within me like a growing tide.

This feels like a final goodbye, like after this date, she'll be forever lost to me.

The dam breaks. A flood of smothering fear makes the words rise to my tongue as if of their own will.

"Lily, don't go."

It's a plea to give herself to me, if only for tonight.

Where is my faith? Where is my commitment to my future wife? They've drifted away like a half-remembered dream, slipping farther from my grasp each time I reach for them.

"What?" she asks with her back to me.

"Don't go." The words are a rasp. "Please."

She turns around, her eyes wide. "I already asked you if I should go. You said yes. You even told me you were proud of me."

I shut my eyes tightly. "Why did you ask me?"

She inhales a sharp breath. "I don't know. I guess because I was trying to understand you. You kissed me weeks ago and promised it would never happen again. Then you kissed me again last night. What does it mean? Were they both mistakes?" She crosses her arms over her chest. "If you want me to cancel my date, you need to give me a damn good reason."

I shatter inside, splitting into two people. One is full of a dark, aching need, desperate to keep her close, to make her mine in every possible way. The other is furious with the inconstancy she pointed out, that my integrity has seemed to slip through my fingers.

My body and my soul call out for her, but my will is stronger. I've proved that, haven't I? I've denied myself so many pleasures over the years, all in service to my faith.

But what has my faith ever given me? Nothing but a rote, lifeless existence.

My resolve crumbles like dry earth under the sun. Years of self-control flow out of me in a rush, and a radiant warmth spreads through my veins.

I close the distance between us in two long strides. My hands find the soft curves of her arms, and I yank her against me.

The kiss is not gentle. It's a storm unleashed. My tongue rubs against hers in a frenzy as I explore the depths of her mouth. My hands roam down her hips, pulling her against me. She moans against my lips, sending a surge of electricity from my gut to the tips of my fingers and toes.

She breaks the kiss suddenly and stares up into my eyes.

My knees buckle. I steady myself and rest my chin on the top of her head. "Stay with me," I murmur. "For the night."

Her breathing is unsteady, but not as ragged as mine. I sense the hesitation in her, the indecision.

"What do you mean, Ethan?"

"Stay with me." My throat catches. "In my bed. *Our* bed."

She grows utterly still, her chest rising and falling in shallow breaths. "You say it's our bed, but you didn't share it with me last night."

"I wanted to." I lift my hand and stroke her cheek. "And I want to now. More than anything." I flinch. "Shit."

What am I doing? I'm practically begging her to sleep with me when I'm not sure if she's ready for such a big step after what Mason did? "Sorry, I'm not thinking straight. I only want you to stay with me if it's what you want. If you're ready."

"I am ready." She lifts her hand to my face, and I close my eyes at her touch, leaning into her warmth. "But are you? If you mean what I think you do...you'd be sinning."

"It might be a sin," I say. "But I want to do it anyway."

Her eyes grow hooded. She lifts onto her toes and presses a soft kiss on my lips. "Alright then. I'll stay."

She pulls out her phone, and her fingers move rapidly over the small keyboard. A blue bubble rises onto the screen. "It's done," she says. "Poor Jake is figuring out his date is extremely flaky, but it's okay. He would have learned eventually." She smiles lazily. "I would have slept with you days ago if you had asked."

Her words fracture my last vestiges of doubt. With trembling hands, I lift her into my arms and carry her to the bed, the heat of her seeping into my skin. Her phone falls from her hand and thumps on the carpet.

"Thank you," I whisper as I set her down gently. She lies back, her bright hair spreading over my pillow. She looks like an angel with her clear-gray eyes and delicate features.

The corners of her lips lift into a sweet smile. "You're welcome."

My hands shake as I reach for the hem of her dress. I peel the fabric away, lifting it over her head. The room is quiet, my ragged breaths the only sound.

When I finally see her bare, my heart stops beating.

Her skin glows like moonlight, her small tits shapely and round with delicious pink nipples. Every curve and line of her body calls to something deep inside, like I've been aching to touch her for a thousand years.

"Lily," I rasp.

Her lips quirk. "Now it's your turn to take your clothes off."

I shake my head sharply. "Not yet."

I want to drink her in first.

After sitting down on the bed, I grab her thighs and spread them apart, revealing her pink, glistening pussy. My gaze is locked, as if she might disappear like a fleeting dream.

"Beautiful."

I want to worship every inch of her. Starting now.

I lower my mouth between her legs, her scent both sweet and earthy. It grows only stronger when my mouth hits her skin.

Her taste is intoxicating.

As my tongue traces the outline of her folds up to her clit, her body trembles, and she lets out a low moan. Her hips buck, and I grip them tightly.

"Oh God, Ethan."

Her words fill me with a dark, aching need. I want more. I need to drink my fill before this exquisite pleasure is out of my reach forever.

She whimpers, filling my chest with an unbearable pressure. I jerk back, panting.

"I think we might..." I swallow. "I need to take this slow."

She smiles dreamily. "Take all the time you need."

I lift myself off the bed and pull my shirt over my head, dying to feel the heat of her skin against mine. When I pull my pants down, my cock springs out. I look up to find Lily staring at it, her eyes wide. "Oh, wow." Her voice is raspy. "You really are a big guy."

Even in this otherworldly state of longing, she can make me smile. "Please stop staring at it. Just tasting you made me...really wound up."

Wound up. What a trivial way to describe the closest I've ever come to heaven. I can almost feel my need for God draining from my body, like a candle flickering out in the dark. A new light fills the void.

Lily. My darling, sassy girl.

"Ethan," she says softly.

"What?" my voice is choked.

"I know how it is for a guy on his first time. I was a virgin once, too. You don't have to worry about how long you last. We have all night."

All night.

All night buried in her heat. If God strikes me down in the morning, it will be worth it.

"Thank you," I say.

I take a step toward the bed and then halt when a thought occurs to me. "Shit, Lily. I don't have a condom."

She waves a hand. "I've been on birth control since high school to keep my periods regular. I've also been to the gyno since...the last time, so I know I'm clean."

When I nod, her eyes glint with mischief. "You'll like how it feels without a condom."

I groan. "I'm going to like how it feels no matter what."

What an understatement. Pleasure is already shooting

through my veins from just looking at her. As I lay my body down on hers, the connection of our skin is electric. She's so damn soft. I shift to the side so I can more easily touch her.

I roam my hands over her, wanting to commit every inch of her to memory so I'll have something to keep me warm during the desolate nights of my uncertain future. I trace my fingers down her neck and over her collarbone. When I reach the delicious swell of her breast, I rub my thumb over her nipple.

She sighs. "That feels good."

I stare down at the pink bud. It's as pretty as a flower.

My hand travels down over her soft belly and into the crease between her legs. She spreads them open to give me access, and I rub my finger over her folds. The wetness makes me hiss, and arrows of pleasure shoot through my limbs.

"Fuck, I need you now." A bead of perspiration trickles down my temple. "Please tell me you're ready for me. I might die if I can't be inside you soon."

She smiles, reaching her hand up and stroking my hair. "I'm ready, big guy."

Big guy. A nickname that usually warms me but now fills me with a dark, heady possessiveness. What she means is I'm *her* big guy. Only hers.

And she's mine.

All mine.

I hoist my body up and crawl over her. The mattress sinks underneath my weight. When I grab my cock and try to guide myself inside her, my hands are shaking, making me clumsy.

She reaches between our hips and wraps her hand around me, her soft touch sending electricity into my gut. "Let me." She positions my cock at her entrance, and I start to push forward.

Oh, holy fuck.

Her searing heat sends a shockwave through my whole body. My soul is consumed by wickedness. I want to crush her. Fill her with my come and mark her as mine forever. I shut my eyes tightly, willing myself to calm down.

I have to be soft with her. If I bring back even the faintest memory of the last time she did this, I'd never forgive myself.

"I trust you, big guy," she croons, as if reading my mind. "Don't hold back."

"You feel like heaven," I say breathlessly.

"So do you."

As I move deeper inside her, pleasure coils inside me like a spring. She's so tight and hot. With one last thrust, I'm fully inside.

The world turns to color like fireworks exploding against a dark sky.

"Jesus Christ," I grit out. "I can't stand it. It's too much."

She lifts her hand to my face. "Give in to it, Ethan. Don't hold back."

When she swivels her hips against mine, my head is pulled down into something dark and primitive. Instinct takes over. I pull my cock almost all the way out from within her and bring my hips crashing back. "You're mine."

"Yes," she pants.

"I'll never let you go." Another thrust. "This is sacred, what we're doing. You belong to me now."

A deep, distant voice tells me my words are that of a madman, but I couldn't stop if I tried. I'm no longer me, but a creature shaped by the pulse of ancient forces.

"Yes, Ethan. I belong to you."

A tidal wave of ecstasy washes over me, and a roar resonates through the room.

Mine, I realize moments later.

"I need more," I say, still panting. "I want to fuck you all night long."

She giggles, a sweet, musical sound. "Your wish is my command, oh lord and master."

Chapter Twenty-Two

L ily

Ethan tightens his grip around my waist, lifts his hips, and thrusts inside me, each movement deliberate and powerful. I'm perched above him, straddling his lap on the couch. He's so damn strong, he's been able to do most of the work—lifting me up and down like he's using my weight to do squats.

His gaze is locked on mine, fierce, almost predatory. "Am I being too rough?" he asks through clenched teeth.

A gasp escapes me as pleasure jolts through my core. "No," I say.

His fingers dig into my skin, pulling me tightly against him, sending arrows of heat through my limbs. I move against his body in a rhythm that has become achingly familiar already.

He likes soft, rolling motions in my hips. I figured that out during our last fucking session against the kitchenette.

This man is insatiable, as if he's trying to quench an endless thirst. This is now our fourth time, and purple morning light is starting to creep into the room.

I should have known. Not only is this Ethan's first night of sex, but he's a star athlete. His endurance is almost infinite. Each time he's lasted longer than before.

He was apologetic over coming so quickly our first time. He didn't know how flattering it was. The last time I was touched, I was treated like a faceless object of pleasure. A vessel to fulfill the needs of a man who never saw me as a whole person.

Ethan looked at me like he was seeing a sunrise for the first time. He was dazzled, reverent.

It's also remarkable how well he's been able to learn my body given his inexperience. He seems to read my thoughts with his intense, dark-blue gaze.

He thrusts harder, and my body bounces on his lap. He slides his hand down my lower back, wrapping his fingers around my ass before delivering a tight squeeze. One finger slides between my cheeks and slips inside my tight hole.

The shriek I let out is a mixture of shock and pleasure. "Holy fuck, Ethan."

"Sorry." His body grows still, and concern flashes across his features.

"Don't be sorry," I pant. "I liked it."

"Good," he grits out. "You have a beautiful ass. So pretty and round. I want to lick it later."

Breathless laughter vibrates from my chest. "I can't believe you. You're ravenous."

He halts his thrusts, searching my face. "Is it too much?

My chest swells with tenderness. He's been checking in with me since we started, clearly anxious that I'm thinking about the last time I had sex.

The truth is those memories hold no power over me. They haven't intruded my brain or hijacked my body's instincts. It's like Ethan is able to erase them when he touches me.

It's because I trust him. This unfailingly principled man would never hurt me.

I lift my hand to his cheek. "No," I whisper. "It's perfect. Almost...healing."

He searches my face. "So you don't mind if I get a little rough with you?"

"I'd love it."

Ethan's response is a growl, feral and hungry, and then he's moving. With our bodies joined, he carries me around the side of the couch. He pulls me off his cock, sets me down, and bends me over the armrest. "Hands down," he commands. "Bend as far forward as you can."

I hesitate for a moment to process his words. My brain is foggy from staying up so late. Crazy that I used to live in this state all the time.

A loud slap resonates through the room, and a sting settles over my ass, like tiny needles pricking my skin.

"Move, Greenwood."

I smile. He's been using that stern coach voice with me on and off throughout the night.

Fuck, it turns me on.

Which is why I'll stay exactly where I am. I peek over my shoulder at him. "No."

He frowns at first, as if confused, but then understanding seems to dawn. The corner of his lips curl into a devilish grin.

"Well, then." His voice is soft and smooth. "I guess you're asking for that spanking over my lap."

An almost hysterical giggle bubbles from my chest. How is it possible that I'm about to get spanked in the nude by my over-bearing protector Ethan Harrington?

"I think you've always wanted to do this," I say. "Every time you got mad at me."

"You're damn right I did." He grabs me by the waist and scoops me into his arms. "It's about time, too. You've been begging for this for years."

He flips me over his lap, and my stomach presses against his hard thighs. His hand brushes over the skin on my ass. "Beautiful," he mutters before giving me a pinch so hard it makes me squeal. "I can't wait to see what it'll look like all red."

My whole body grows tense. "Oh my God, Ethan. You're killing me. Just do it already."

He laughs darkly. "No, not yet. I'm savoring the moment." He rubs circles over one ass cheek. "It's going to hurt, my sassy girl," he croons, "but it's for your own good."

I laugh breathlessly. "My God, you are kinky for a virgin."

He pinches my skin again. "I'm not a virgin anymore. Alright, here we go."

His palm leaves my skin suddenly, and I brace myself for impact.

It doesn't come.

"You're torturing me," I say.

"I sure am."

A moment later, his hand lands hard on my right cheek, and a jolt of pain shoots through me. I yelp, my hands flying to my stinging ass. "Holy shit, that was hard."

"Are you okay, baby?" His voice is as gentle as an ocean breeze, a sweet contrast to his sternness moments before.

"Yes," I gasp, warmth filling my belly. "I liked it."

"Good, because that was..." He groans, his hard cock jerking against my belly. "Real fucking satisfying for me."

He slaps me again, even harder this time. "That was for taking all your clothes off in my frat."

SLAP!

"That was for all the guys you've kissed right in front of me."

SLAP!

"And that was for being so goddamn tempting all these years. Torturing me with that sassy mouth of yours."

My ass is on fire, and liquid seeps from my pussy. I whimper. "I want more."

"No. You're going to ask for my forgiveness for all the years you made me hard against my will."

Arrows of heat shoot through my veins. Oh God, why couldn't we have done this years ago?

"I'm sorry, Ethan. Please forgive me.

He runs his fingers through my hair. "Not like that. It's time for you to apologize with your body."

My tummy flips over as he picks me up and strides over to the wall. After pressing my back against the cool surface, he shoves himself inside me in one piercing thrust. His hips drive into mine with renewed intensity.

"Fuck, you're so perfect," he hisses, shutting his eyes tightly as if in pain. "I'm about to explode after spanking that gorgeous ass."

"Let go, big guy," I whisper.

"Not yet. I need you there, too."

I shake my head, my muscles trembling. "I can't. It feels so good, but...I think I'm spent."

His eyes flash. "We'll see about that."

I want to laugh at his determination. I was so right about what he would be like in bed. He's as intent on my pleasure as he is about every other goal in his life.

He slides his hand down the curve of my belly until he finds my clit. "Show me how you like it," he rasps. "Quick."

His command sends a jolt through me, reigniting embers in my belly I thought had burned out. After grabbing his fingers, I guide them up and down against my clit.

I'm not sure if it's the heat of Ethan's eyes or the sensation of the rough pads of his fingers against my clit, but the fire in my belly is building to a blaze. His hips are moving fast, pushing my body up the wall. My eyelids flutter closed, and pleasure coils tighter.

"You're so beautiful," he says. "I swear, just looking at you could make me come."

His words make stars flare against the blackness behind my

eyelids, and then it hits me, an eruption of pleasure seizes my body in a vise. My back arches against the cool wall, and I cry out as waves of ecstasy ripple through my whole body.

Distantly, through the haze, I hear Ethan's own groan of release. It's a guttural sound. A hot rush of liquid fills my insides.

My limbs slacken, and Ethan collapses against me, but his hold on my hips is as firm as ever. We stay against the wall for who knows how long, the world blurring as my breathing begins to steady.

"I love coming inside you," Ethan says.

I'm pulled out of my languid daze, craning my neck to look at him. His face is flushed, and sweat is beaded on his brow. "You do?" I ask.

His chest rises and falls against mine. He lifts his gaze to meet mine. "I don't quite understand it, but I love filling you with a part of me." His eyes darken. "It makes me feel like you belong to me. I know it sounds crazy."

I smooth a lock of damp hair away from his forehead. "It's not crazy. I like feeling like you belong to me, too."

He searches my face, his eyes intense, the fierceness from earlier softened into something more tender, more vulnerable. "Am I pushing you too hard?" he asks. "I've been fucking you all night. I don't want you to feel like...it's all about me. Tell me what you want."

I lift my hand to his cheek. "Tonight has been perfect. You've made sure of that."

He doesn't say anything, but the relief that floods his face tells me everything I need to know.

This man prioritizes my needs. Even when he's ravenous for sex after years of deprivation, he can't stop thinking about what happened to me six months ago and what I might be feeling and might need.

I don't think I've ever met a man like him before. My God, have I accepted the bare minimum from men all my life because I've never known any better? I'm not the type of woman to let a man treat me like shit. So why does Ethan's sweet treatment make me feel like I've stepped into another world?

Ethan lifts my spent body from the wall and carries me back to the bed. After laying me down gently, he strides over to the kitchenette.

I marvel at the sight of him. That firm ass and those rippling muscles on his back. I never thought he'd be so relaxed in the nude, but then again, he must know he's a beautiful physical specimen.

He grabs a towel from the counter and turns on the faucet.

"Ethan," I say. "I don't need to be cleaned up."

He shakes his head as he turns to me and starts walking back to the bed. "My come is dripping down your thigh." His lips quirk. "As much as I love the sight of it, it's got to be uncomfortable. Plus..." He sits down on the bed, and the mattress dips under his weight. "I like taking care of you."

The affectionate glint in his eyes warms my whole body. It's a look that says he would do anything to ensure my comfort. His touch is careful and precise as he cleans me up. It's endearing, so characteristically Ethan. When he's finished, he bunches the towel into a ball and sends it through the air like a rocket. It lands in the center of the laundry basket at the other end of the room.

"Show off," I murmur, my eyes starting to fall shut.

He climbs into the bed and pulls my face against his chest. "If that was showing off, I'm in serious trouble. I thought I fucked your brains out tonight. I hope you weren't faking those orgasms."

"Fucked my brains out," a soft voice says. "Yes. It was the best...ever."

"Really?" someone murmurs.

In the next moment, I drift into peaceful oblivion.

<h1 style="text-align:center">Chapter Twenty-Three</h1>

E ^{than}

Morning sunlight brushes over her face, casting streaks of shadows from her lashes over her cheekbones. That bright-red hair fans out over the pillow. Her lips are slightly parted, pink, and a little swollen from my kisses.

She's the most beautiful thing I've ever seen, and she's mine.

A buzzing energy courses through my veins, almost like a high. I haven't slept a wink. This is maybe the first time since I was a kid that I stayed up all night.

I understand now how people become addicted to sex. The fireworks of pumping and exploding inside of her were exquisite enough, but the heady possessiveness that settled over me afterward was much longer lasting.

She belongs to me.

Only me.

And where is the guilt? I thought for sure it would settle in after the euphoria of coming inside her faded. Yet, I haven't felt even a twinge of it yet.

It's as if God has disappeared.

I clench my jaw. If he refuses to reach out to me, I won't cry about it. I've called out to him so many times over the years, begged for his comfort. All he ever gave me was a deep, unshakable guilt, an ever-present reminder of my unworthiness.

God, if you want me to give up the paradise on earth I've found, you need to try a little harder. Show me your unconditional love and forgiveness. Until you do...

I'm going to savor every precious moment with Lily.

I reach out and rub my thumb along her full bottom lip. God, she's gorgeous. What would it be like to wake up to this every day?

I never understood the phrase "heaven on earth" until now. This girl has shattered everything I thought I knew. Fucking her brought me into a realm of quiet wonder and profound peace.

Why have I only ever felt it with her? It's the kind of experience that should only come from God. Or so I always believed.

It doesn't make sense that sin could feel so...freeing.

I lean down, my lips finding the warmth of her skin. I trace the line of her shoulder with gentle kisses. She stirs underneath me, a soft moan escaping her lips.

A delicious sound.

"Lily," I whisper against her neck, "you have class in an hour."

Her body stiffens, and she bolts upright, her body jarring into my face.

I put my hand over my nose. "Ow," I say, but it doesn't hurt.

Nothing could hurt me in the state I'm in. It's as if I have opium pumping through my veins.

"It's Thursday." Her voice thick with sleep. "Your political theory class is before mine."

"I missed it," I say.

Her expression changes from sleepy to incredulous. "You missed a class?"

I smile at her shock. "It was just a Q and A session for an exam."

She continues to frown at me. "You ditched?"

"I lost my virginity last night. Isn't that even more out of character for me than skipping a single class?"

Her eyes grow unfocused, as if she's drifting into a daze. "It is," she mutters. "Do you feel terrible?"

"No," I say immediately. "I feel great."

She blinks several times, and I stroke the soft strands of hair at her temple. I stare into her stormy-gray eyes, wishing she could see my soul in mine. I want her to know how much I meant what I said.

I don't regret what I did. It's up to God now. I'm playing chicken with him. It's his turn to strike back. He has to fill my heart with guilt before I'll give this up.

He will, eventually. It's inevitable.

But for now, I'm giving in to bliss.

"Why don't you skip class?" I ask. "Let's go do something."

A saucy smile tugs at her lips. "Does it involve a bed?"

My gut clenches as I press a soft kiss against her jawline. "Later. I don't want to wear you out. Let's go to the beach or something. I'll need you fully recovered before tonight."

She's quiet for a long while. Her gray eyes darting back and forth as if she's lost in thought. "Ethan..."

"What?" I ask, anxiety gripping my chest.

"Last night was magical," she says, "but I'm worried about you."

I release the breath I was holding. "Why are you worried about me?"

She lifts her hand and strokes my hair, and I lean into the touch. "This isn't like you," she says. "You've had women throwing themselves at you for years. I've seen it at parties. You've never seemed to have any trouble...keeping your chastity pledge. You threw it all away for me, and now you don't feel bad about it?"

Because I'm falling for you, Lily.

Fuck, I can't say it, even though I'm dying to know if she feels the same way. I can't make any declarations that might promise a future. It sure feels like God abandoned me today, but what if he fills my heart with guilt tomorrow?

I'm lost at sea, my faith as elusive as the stars behind the clouds.

And I can't bring myself to care.

I poke the tip of her nose with my finger. She has such a cute nose, just like the rest of her. "I don't know why I don't feel bad," I say, "but I'm living in the moment for once. Something that's easy for my sassy girl, so can you indulge me?"

"Yes," she mutters. "For now."

I don't like the sound of "for now" on her lips. I want her to tell me that she's mine forever. I want to be the one she leans on, the one she trusts, the one she can't imagine her life without.

It's crazy. She doesn't even want to get married. That alone should be my sign from God that Lily and I are doomed.

"Great," I say to clear my head. "Let's go to the beach."

She sighs. "Well, I'll be skipping painting studio, and I need to get something done. Why don't you let me sketch you?" Her smile grows mischievous. "I can make you the subject of my final project. My classmates will recognize you, and they'll think I've become one of Ethan Harrington's many groupies. They'll pity me, thinking I could never land the golden boy. Oh God, I love it."

Warmth spreads through my chest. Fuck, she's adorable. I love how unselfconsciously silly she is. "I can't imagine loving being the subject of ridicule, but I'm happy to lend myself to your cause."

"I love it because we're keeping a secret." A wicked glint appears in her eyes. "It's like we have our own little world, just the two of us. No one else gets to see this side of you. Just me."

Possessiveness crashes over me like a tidal wave. Maybe she does feel the same way I do.

She's mine. Only mine.

And I belong to her.

* * *

"Right there, Ethan. Perfect."

Lily's eyes sparkle as she takes out a notebook from her woven bag. She's been in her element since we started scouting locations for her sketches. I've never seen her so serious, so authoritative. When I plop down on the sand, her gaze narrows on my face. She sets the charcoal pencil to paper.

She moves quickly, each stroke on the pad fluid and featherlight. Her brow pinches ever so slightly as she glances back and forth between me and the paper. Whenever she looks at my face, her gaze is so intent, so probing, it makes my cock stir.

"Fuck, Lily. I don't think I can sit like this for long with you staring at me. I want to throw you back on the sand and have my way with you."

She frowns, picks up a scoop of sand, and tosses it in my direction. "You're insatiable. I'm actually sore from last night."

My pulse starts to pound. "Oh shit, really? I didn't mean to... You should have told me. I wouldn't have kept going if I knew—"

"Stop, Ethan." She rolls her eyes. "You're the sweetest, most considerate man I've ever met. I am sore, but it's not a bad thing. In fact, it turns me on. Especially the pain on my ass. It reminds me of everything we did last night."

Electricity shoots into my gut as visceral memories flood through my senses—the slapping sound of her skin as she bounced on my lap, the sight of her plump ass red with the print of my hand.

Fuck, I want her now.

"You're looking at me like you're ready to eat me," she says.

I groan. "I am ready to eat you. It sucks having to just sit here and not touch you. How about we take a quick break?" I pat my thigh. "I only need a few kisses. Maybe somewhere a little more exotic than your pretty mouth..."

She laughs, and it's a sweet musical sound. "I can't believe you. We're in public."

I glance over my shoulder at the beach. A lone jogger strides across the wet sand near the water. "We're alone. Mostly."

She shakes her head, sketching what looks like the shape of my jaw. "I'm a bad influence on you. You're becoming a degenerate. Imagine what would happen if we were caught having sex in public. It would probably end up on the news."

I shake my head. "I'm too competitive. I'd make it my mission to make you come without getting caught."

Her eyes grow huge. "Stop. I need to get this sketch done. It's technically your job to help me improve my grades, Mr. Harrington. What would Noah think if he knew my accountability partner fucked my brains out last night?" She winces. "Sorry. I don't mean to make you feel guilty."

Strangely, she didn't. Not only has God abandoned me, but so has my loyalty to Noah.

I don't even know myself.

"*I* don't feel guilty, by the way," Lily says. "Noah's rule that no teammates can touch his sister is gross. It feels like you were always meant to touch me."

"Me too. Somehow it feels like..." I twist around and stare out at the ocean. The afternoon sun is like diamonds over the water. A deep, soothing tranquility settles over me. "I don't know. I wanted you for years, and now...all is finally right with the world. Does that make any sense?"

Her pencil drops to the sand. When I glance up, her gray eyes are fixed on my face. "What do you mean *years*?" Her voice is quiet.

I frown. Is it really so surprising to her after everything that's happened in the last twenty-four hours?

"I wanted you from the moment I laid eyes on you. I didn't

understand it fully—or maybe I was just in deep denial. But a part of me always knew. I think that's why I've been so protective but distant at the same time. You were off-limits as Noah's little sister, and…it's uncomfortable wanting something you can't have."

Her dazed expression makes me chuckle. "Why do you seem so shocked? My brother and sister-in-law have been making fun of me for years over you. They knew I wanted you before I did."

She gasps. "So you… You talked about me to them?"

"I did. I told my whole family you needed God. I was a self-righteous prick. That's why I practically forced you to come to Thanksgiving last year even when you said you were just fine spending it with a few of your sorority sisters who didn't go home." I laugh humorlessly. "I was trying to show you God's love."

Fuck, I was so stupid. The truth is I've never met anyone who needs God less than Lily. She's so free, not bound by guilt or fear like I've been my whole life.

She laughs. "Showing me God's love by basically demanding I spend Thanksgiving with your family. You're adorable, Ethan."

The tension leaves my shoulders in an instant. I love how accepting she is of my flaws. I've never felt as comfortable in my own skin as when I'm around her.

"I was deluding myself," I say. "I told myself you needed to be saved by God because it gave me an excuse to keep guys away from you when I got jealous." I smile ruefully. "I was saving you on God's behalf."

"You kind of hinted at that, but I never knew." Her expression grows thoughtful. "When were you jealous?"

I scoff. "Millions of times. Do you remember that night you had three guys surrounding you at a bar, and I had Brandon pretend to be your boyfriend to get you away from them?"

She laughs. "Three guys? You're remembering it wrong. I'm pretty sure it was only one. You always seemed to think I was a much bigger partier than I really was."

I snort. "It was absolutely three guys. Trust me. I was the jealous one. Anyway, one of them made you laugh. It was so loud I heard it from across the restaurant. I knew it was you before I even saw your face. No one else has that laugh. It's so...uninhibited. I had to get those guys away from you. I think it was because..." My eyes lock onto hers. "I wanted that laughter to belong to me. I wanted you to be mine, even though I didn't know it yet."

She swallows. "Ethan, what does this mean?"

My chest fills with a delicious warmth. Is she asking what I think she is? Does she want to belong to me as much as I want to belong to her?

I can't tell her the truth—that right now, I'd sacrifice anything to keep her. Anything.

Eventually, the guilt will have to settle in—the conviction that I've crossed a line and have to repent. There's no way it won't. I've betrayed my best friend and all my values. I've betrayed my future wife.

I want my future wife to be Lily, goddamn it. In the moment, it feels like I could commit murder to make it happen.

But that's not what she wants. Marriage isn't for her.

I refuse to try to change her. She's perfect just as she is.

"I don't know," I say. "I'm sorry that I can't give you a better answer than that."

She nods slowly, her gaze fixed on her sketch. "Do you mind if we..." She rubs her hand across her forehead, creating a gray smudge from the charcoal on her fingers. "I'm getting a bit of a headache."

My stomach drops. "Are you upset about what I just said?"

"No. I know having sex for the first time was a big deal for you. I don't expect you to understand what it all means right away. I'm honestly not feeling great. I think maybe I've had too much sun."

I look at her closely, my skepticism growing. Her cheeks are flushed, and there's a slight glaze to her eyes that wasn't there before. "Too much sun?" I ask. "It's not that hot."

She shakes her head. "I think I'm just tired. You have practice this afternoon, right? I'll take a nap while you're gone." She smiles lazily. "Then I'll be rested for tonight."

Heat shoots into my gut. "Tonight is too far away. Can you make time move faster?"

Chapter Twenty-Four

E^{than}

"Ethan!" Coach Rodriguez shouts. "Are you sleepwalking out there?"

The sun drills into my eyes, and my head pounds, and I try to increase my speed, but my legs feel like they have weights attached to them. My footwork is atrocious as I weave through the cones, misjudging the distances and stumbling slightly with each abrupt turn.

It's from lack of sleep, but it was worth it.

"Move, Ethan, move!" Coach Rodriguez's shout snaps me back to the present, to the pathetic display of my body refusing to cooperate.

God, how did Lily survive months without sleep? I'm ready to collapse after a single night without it. I'll probably need a nap if I plan to fuck her all night again.

"Practice is over for you, Harrington." Coach Rodriguez's

voice makes me jump. "Hit the shower. I can't watch any more of this. It's pathetic."

I shut my eyes and inhale a deep breath. Oh, well. It's just one practice. And it means I'll get to come home to Lily sooner.

"I'm not feeling well today," I say to coach, but it's a lie.

I feel better than I have in my whole life, like I've tuned into a higher frequency of existence.

Coach crosses his arms over his chest. "Oh, really? I never would have guessed."

"I just need a full night's sleep."

But I won't get it.

"You need to avoid getting drunk," he says. "At least until the end of the season."

I frown. "I'm not hungover."

Coach rolls his eyes. "You think I haven't seen this before? I expect it from the other guys, but not you. Do you have any idea, the position you're in? How lucky you are?" He pulls his phone from his pocket. "Let me show you something."

I already know what he's about to show me. Some sports commentator critiquing my performance.

I fight the urge to roll my eyes. I shouldn't be snapping at him, even if he did just wrongly accuse me of being hungover. It was a reasonable assumption, and in a way, I was drunk last night.

Drunk on Lily.

Coach presses play on his phone, and sure enough, a commentator starts talking. "The pressure is on this season for Harrington. He's got to prove that he can do this on a consistent basis."

"Do you understand what's at stake here?" Coach asks.

"I do," I say firmly.

"I don't think that's true," he says. "You won the jackpot last year, Harrington. No one would have any idea who you are if it wasn't for your incredible performance against Redwood State. Division II wide receivers don't usually have scouts knocking on their door."

I nod. "I understand. I really do." The words are hollow, even to my own ears. "It's just...I've got stuff going on."

"Stuff," he scoffs. "We've all got stuff going on. But how many of us have a shot like yours?" His eyes lock onto mine. "Get out of here. You'd better look alive tomorrow."

"Understood," I say before turning around and heading toward the locker room.

As I make my way off the field toward the benches, Mason, who just finished a drill, steps in front of me, his grin as sharp as ever.

Fuck. I've been using all my focus to forget his existence, but he seems to take any opportunity he can to taunt me.

What a fucking idiot. It's almost like he wants to get pummeled.

"How's Lily doing?" he drawls loud enough for everyone around to hear.

Anger flares up inside me, like it always does when he talks about her. How dare he. He ought to be wasting away in jail, not wanting to even think of her, let alone mention her name.

I take a deep breath, trying to think of a measured response. I glance over my shoulder to make sure Noah isn't within earshot. Thankfully, he's yards away doing a tackling drill with the linebackers. I turn back to Mason, clenching my jaw. "Keep her name out of your mouth."

Mason's eyes grow huge. "Oh, damn. She really got to you, didn't she? Careful. Don't let her get too close. You don't want her making wild accusations that could ruin your whole football career just because she's desperate for attention."

An unholy rage fizzes through my veins, distorting the world around me. I retreat into my head in an attempt to calm myself.

Don't hit him, Ethan. Lily wouldn't want you to.

I take a step in his direction, lowering my chin, and shooting him a glare. "I know exactly who you are." My voice is as quiet as the dead. "Believe me when I say you don't want to push me,

Mason. Cemeteries are full of people who thought they were invincible."

His face leaches of color. "Holy, shit. A death threat from the Christian virgin." He shakes his head. "She's got you by the balls. You're in for rude awakening. She's a fucking liar, and you're gonna find out—"

I turn on my heel and walk away, my anger burning like an inferno in my chest. I can't listen to him any longer, or I will hit him.

My quick shower does nothing to calm me, and my thoughts are still racing on the drive home. But as soon as I pull up in front of the frat house, the tension in my body starts to ebb.

Fuck, I love coming home to her.

When I jog up the steps of our porch, I'm startled by the sight of Lily. She's sitting at the wicker table with a sketchbook in front of her. Aiden is sitting across from her, and she's staring at his face as she brushes pencil strokes across the paper. He's grinning at her like she's the most adorable person in the world.

Jealousy rises like a storm within me, but I try to tamp it down. She *is* the most adorable person in the world, and I'm the man who gets to fuck her. Drawing and painting is what gives her life meaning, and it has nothing to do with me.

Crazy that I want every part of her to belong to me and only me. I never thought I was this possessive.

"Did you take a nap?" I ask Lily, my voice a touch sharper than I'd intended.

"Aiden begged me for a sketch." She smiles lazily. Her eyes are unusually bright, and her face is flushed like it was on the beach. "I swindled him out of three-hundred bucks for it."

"Swindled?" Aiden's brows draw together, though he's still smiling devilishly at her—the bastard. "You said that's the going rate."

"I lied," she says. "But don't worry, I'll embellish your features and make you better looking. It's my job to..." Her brow knits, and her eyes grow unfocused. "Shit. What was I saying?"

My gaze roams over her face. Something about her is off. She looks almost...feverish. When I catch sight of her shaking fingers, I snap into action. I march over and put my hand on her forehead. The skin under my hand is as hot as a stove. "Holy shit, Lily. You're burning up."

She looks at me with a confused frown. Then she chuckles, but it's not her usual abandoned laughter. Fuck, I don't like this. She's not herself.

"Come on," I say, grabbing her hand. "I'm putting you to bed."

She stares at me for a long moment, as if processing my words slowly. "But...Aiden's sketch."

"You can finish it later," Aiden says, now standing by the front door. "I don't want any of those germs. Fuck, I hope I didn't catch them already." A moment later, he disappears inside the house.

"Oh no," Lily mutters, staring at me with glazed eyes. "You might catch it too. I should go back to my sorority..."

I cross my arms over my chest and shoot her a stern expression. "You will not. I'm taking care of you. It's too late for me already." My lips quirk as I lower my voice. "I don't know if you remember, but I had my mouth all over you last night. And this morning."

Her eyes grow hooded. "You sure did, big guy. Ready for another marathon? Mama needs her loving." She slaps her hand over her mouth and bursts into breathless giggles. "Mama. Loving. I've never used those words before. How cringe."

Fuck, she's acting weird. She seems almost drunk. Her fever must be really high.

"I'm not having sex with you when you're sick." I grab her hand and pull her up from her chair. When she's finally standing, she wobbles a little. Anxiety prickles over my skin. Her eyes grow wide as I scoop her into my arms.

"My knight in shining armor." Her head lolls against my shoulder, alarming me further.

"Your knight is about to take your temperature—" I carry her through the front door "—and if it's as high as I think it is, he's making you go to the campus clinic. No arguments."

She scoffs "Ethan, you're acting crazy. It's just a fever. I refuse to let you torture me when I'm already not feeling good."

"Too bad. If it's any higher than 102, you're going."

When we make it to my bedroom, I rush over to the bed and lay her down gently. A lazy smile tugs at her lips. "Are you afraid I'm going to die, Ethan?"

My mouth drops open, and she bursts into giggles. "Oh my God, you really are."

I scowl at her, irritation flaring in my veins. "People die of the flu, Lily. People even die of the common cold. It's rare, but it happens."

Her expression grows pitying, but I'm not even a little embarrassed for saying something so outrageous. I don't want to think about Lily dying, even if the chances are extremely remote.

I need her like I need to breathe.

"Come here," Lily says, gesturing at the bed. "I have something I need to tell you."

I frown in confusion but follow her direction. When I sit down next to her, she reaches out and takes my hand. Her skin is clammy, giving me another flare of anxiety.

Her expression grows grave. "There will be no sappy songs played at my funeral. I want bangers only. In fact, the whole thing needs to be a dance party. Why aren't you writing this down? These are my final wishes."

The tension in my body eases at her joke, and warmth fills me everywhere. God, she's cute. I thought I was good in a crisis, always able to take action, but it turns out, Lily is even better.

It feels like I've found a missing piece. I make a big deal out of nothing sometimes. It's how I'm wired. It might help my productivity and problem solving, but it certainly doesn't feel good. Lily softens my sharp edges with her silliness and ease.

Fuck. I don't think I'll ever be able to let her go.

I try to shake off the thought as I squeeze her hand. "Only if you come with me to the campus clinic. If not, I'll make sure your funeral is the most depressing thing ever. An old church that smells like mildew. Organ music. Everyone wearing black and sobbing. I'll get up on stage to give a eulogy, and I'll talk about how you lit up a room."

She makes a gagging sound, and I smile.

"But that's not all," I say. "I'll tell them all how your smile made everything brighter, how you always knew how to make me laugh, even on my worst days. I'll say you were the sunshine in my life, and without you, my whole world has turned to darkness." Fuck, what am I doing baring my soul to her? My anxiety over her illness is making me lose my mind. "I'll tell them I was lost before you found me, and how you taught me that I was lacking something profound. Something I didn't even know was missing until you."

Her glazed eyes are fixed on my face. "What?"

I swallow. "Joy."

When she intakes a sharp breath, I drop her hand, and stand up from the bed. What the hell was that? Now is not the time for sappy confessions. I need to take care of her.

"Alright, I'm getting the thermometer." Without looking at her face, I head out of my room and into the kitchen. I grab the first aid kit from a high shelf in the pantry, fumble with the latch, and yank out the digital thermometer. In what feels like a split second later, I'm putting it inside Lily's mouth. My hands shake as I maneuver it under her tongue.

The numbers on the screen shoot up immediately to over a hundred. The wait is agony as they slow and settle on a single number.

One hundred...and four.

My stomach plummets to the floor. "Holy shit, Lily! This is the highest fever I've ever seen."

She sets her hand on my shoulder, and that pitying smile has returned to her face. "My fevers always run high. I can text my mom right now and have her back me up if you're worried. I promise I'm not dying."

I shake my head, my thoughts growing dazed. "I think we should go to the emergency room."

"No." Her voice is sharp.

I turn to her with a scowl. "It might be a sign of something serious...like sepsis. I don't think you understand. This is a really high fever."

She frowns incredulously. "Sepsis? Are you crazy? Ethan, I'm starting to think you might be one of those doomsday people." She glances around my bedroom. "Where are your canned beans?"

Her sass is comforting, a sign that she's still herself. If she were septic, she'd likely be too listless to ridicule me. Still, I'm not good at compromise, but taking her to the ER when she's refusing to cooperate might do more harm than good. Her body needs to rest if she's going to fight off whatever is causing this fever.

"Fine," I say. "We'll go to the clinic."

Chapter Twenty-Five

Lily

Ethan's face is strained as he stares into my eyes. We're standing at an altar on the edge of a cliff overlooking the ocean, and he's wearing a tuxedo.

For some reason, he's also wearing a large, polka-dot bowtie. Who okayed that ugly thing? This is our wedding day, damn it. Why is he dressed like a clown?

"I can't do this," he says, his voice tight. "I sinned, Lily. There's no coming back from sin. This is over. I'm choosing God."

"No," I whimper.

"It's okay, sassy girl." Ethan's voice is now distant, echoing from the sky. The Ethan in front of me blurs and fades away, and I'm pulled into a bright room. My head is pressed against a hard chest. "The doctor should be calling us any minute," Ethan says.

Oh, that's right. We're sitting in the waiting room of the campus clinic.

Damn, I must have fallen asleep. And where did that bizarre dream come from? Ethan would never marry me, even if I wanted to get married in the first place.

It was probably that sweet speech of his messing with my head.

"You taught me that I was lacking something profound. Joy."

Oh God, I think I could marry Ethan. If it really mattered to him, I could compromise. I don't really care much about the institution of marriage—it's just a stupid tradition. But it's deeply meaningful to Ethan, and that matters.

It matters—I think—because I love him.

My burning-hot eyes grow misty. Fuck, this fever is making me crazy.

He sets his hand on my forehead. A notch appears between his thick brows. "You feel a little cooler."

I blink, attempting to focus on his face, but everything is blurred, like I'm looking through murky water. "Then let's go. I hate going to the doctor. I'll have to wait another eternity after they bring me into the room."

His eyes flash with determination. "Then take another nap on my shoulder. I'm not taking you home until you see a doctor."

I want to laugh. He's so stern and commanding, like an army general.

It's hot. He's so damn caring.

And yet, he doesn't even know what he wants from me, and here I was, thinking I could marry him.

Stupid fever.

Ethan stands up and marches toward the front desk. "How much longer?" he asks the attendant. "My girlfriend's getting a little restless."

My stomach flips over. *Girlfriend?*

"The nurse should be calling you any minute," the girl says.

Ethan nods once before returning to his seat.

"Why did you call me your girlfriend?" I ask.

He's quiet for a moment. "I don't know. It just...came out."

My already fuzzy head grows heavier and cloudier. Ethan's never had a girlfriend before. He plans to only ever date his wife.

Did "girlfriend" really just slip out, or does it mean something deeper about his feelings for me?

A sheepish smile tugs his lips. "I'm pretty sure they already think I'm your boyfriend, because I've been acting like an anxious freak."

Warmth washes over me. He is acting like an anxious freak, and I love it. He's really worried about me.

Because I'm important to him.

Ethan's gaze snaps to the open door when a lady appears with a chart in her hand. "Lily?" she calls out, glancing around the room.

When I stand up suddenly, dizziness washes over me, making the room spin. Ethan wraps his arm around my waist and yanks me against his chest.

"I'm coming with my girlfriend." His tone is firm. "She's so out of it, I don't think she'll remember any of the doctor's instructions."

Indignation flares in my veins, and I jerk my head in his direction. "I'm not out of it."

His eyes flash. "You were muttering nonsense when you were sleeping a second ago. I'm coming with you."

Without giving me a chance to respond, he yanks me against his chest, giving me support as a nurse guides us through a hallway. The scent of antiseptic makes my stomach churn.

"Let's check your vitals," the nurse says as she guides me to a chair and wraps a cuff around my arm. A moment later, the cuff inflates tightly and releases.

"Blood pressure is normal," the nurse says.

"Her pulse is high though." Ethan's brow is furrowed as he stares at the screen beside me. "She's been sleeping almost the whole time we've been here. Shouldn't it be lower than that?"

The nurse smiles warmly at Ethan. "It's common with a fever. Her body is working hard to fight off an infection."

"I'm not an athlete," I say. "My pulse is always high."

He rolls his eyes. "Your fevers are always high... Your pulse is always high... Stop bullshitting me, Greenwood. We'll see what the doctor says."

My stomach flips over. Fuck, he's so cute when he's exasperated with me.

A while later, I'm sitting on a paper-covered table while Ethan paces the room. The door opens, and a man in a white coat appears. "Hi Lily," he says with a smile. "I'm Dr. Carter."

He immediately pulls out his stethoscope and places it against my chest. Ethan hovers over him, his brows pulled together. "Her pulse is really fast," he clips out. "Is that normal?"

"With a high fever, yes." Dr. Carter shines a light into my ear. "Do you have any other symptoms, Lily? Any nausea, vomiting, or diarrhea?

"Lots of diarrhea," I say. "Explosive."

Dr. Carter doesn't even flinch. "When did it start?"

Ethan groans. "She's joking. Trying to make me uncomfortable. It's her favorite thing to do."

I shoot Ethan a saucy smile, and he rolls his eyes. God, I'm acting like a child.

The exam is over within ten minutes. As I expected, nothing is seriously wrong with me. Just a virus of some kind.

"Alright, Ethan." Dr. Carter hands Ethan a small slip of paper. "Tylenol every four to six hours, and make sure she drinks plenty of fluids."

"Wow," I murmur. "What a revelation. I have a fever and I need Tylenol. This wasn't a waste of time at all."

Ethan shoots me a stern look before grabbing the note from Dr. Carter's hand. "Are you sure she doesn't need some kind of antibiotic? Her fever was much higher earlier. A hundred and four. What if she has some kind of bacterial infection, like meningitis?"

I suck in my lips to fight my laughter, and based on Dr. Carter's tight expression, I think he might be doing the same.

"Meningitis is rare," he says. "And she doesn't have any other symptoms like a headache or stiff neck. Tylenol should be just fine. Just keep an eye on her temperature." Dr. Carter pats Ethan's shoulder. "If it climbs back up, don't hesitate to bring her back in."

We stand, ready to leave, and I sway slightly, still wobbly on my feet. Ethan catches my elbow, steadying me. His grip is strong—always so strong.

"Take care of her, but remember to look after yourself too," Dr. Carter adds, his eyes twinkling. "It's obvious you're... anxious."

Ethan blushes as he nods. "My girlfriend doesn't get sick very often."

Dr. Carter says something else, but I don't hear the words. My whole body is enveloped in a warm haze.

Ethan didn't have to call me his girlfriend just now. It would have made more sense to call me "Lily" or even "she." He called me his girlfriend because he wanted to say it. Because he likes the sound of it as much as I do.

So I wasn't imagining the hidden emotion in Ethan's slip of the tongue.

It meant something. I just wish I knew what exactly.

Chapter Twenty-Six

E than

She stirs in her sleep, flipping from side to side like a flag fluttering in a storm.

She's been doing that all night long, and I've barely slept a wink. My eyes are as dry as sandpaper. Three times now, she's bolted up in bed and muttered nonsense into the dark room. Each time, I coaxed her to drink water before tucking her back in bed.

I don't mind it at all. After the doctor assured me that nothing is seriously wrong with her, it became my pleasure to take care of her. It feels like my job, and my job alone, like this intimate side of her belongs to only me.

She's mine.

At least for now.

All night, I've been torn by two needs. I have to make sure she's alright. I don't think Lily would be very diligent about following doctor's orders given her spontaneous personality. How many times did she dismiss being sick in the first place?

But a deeper, more melancholy part of me is possessed by the selfish craving to etch every detail of her face into my memory.

I don't know when the guilt will come. It hovers in the distance like a specter, haunting the edges of my consciousness.

I don't want this to end. Fuck, I want to die at the thought alone.

I've always been taught that sin is deceitful. It lures you away from the light by seducing you with empty promises. Guilt has never failed to tug at my heart whenever I'd done something wrong.

But this thing with Lily doesn't feel wrong. It feels like I've finally found the path to my true home.

Lily's head lolls in my direction. Her brow is furrowed, and I brush my thumb across it before setting my hand on her chest. The gentle rise and fall of her breathing is a balm to my restless nerves. I think she's getting better.

She stirs again. "Wh-what time is it?" Her voice is a raspy whisper.

"I think it's around three," I whisper. "Go back to sleep."

Beneath the faint glow of the streetlights seeping through the window, she blinks slowly, her dazed expression ebbing away. "I think...my fever's gone."

"Really?" I press my palm against her forehead, and a smile lifts my lips. She's cool under my touch. "I think you're right. Your fever broke."

"Thank God," she mumbles. "Now you'll stop harassing me to drink water."

Calm floods every part of me. That was my sassy girl speaking just now. Her voice was clear and cutting, so unlike the delirious, incoherent ridicule she's been throwing at me all night.

The idea of her being anything less than her fiery self clawed at my insides.

"Right," I say. "I'm not trying to make sure you get better. I'm vacuuming up your joy."

She snorts and then winces, setting her hand on her forehead.

"My head feels like an elephant sat on it. But overall I feel much better."

"Sleep," I command.

She wrinkles her nose. "Bossy."

"Always."

"I'm not tired..." she mumbles, but her voice drifts off at the end as if she's already falling asleep. I smile. She's so damn stubborn, and I love it.

I feel like I love her, but how could I if this is really a sin? Just two weeks ago, I knew in my soul that I was meant to save myself for my future wife.

Is it her, God? Is that what you're trying to tell me? The thought sends a surge of possessive heat through my whole body.

Fuck, I want it to be true, but it's insane. Lily doesn't want to get married. She views the whole institution of marriage as a loss of freedom for women.

I could never cage her. I would rather stand in awe of her from the sidelines than risk extinguishing her flame.

The thought that she might be my future wife is probably just my tired, aching heart trying to convince myself that I've done nothing wrong. Didn't my dad do the same thing? When he left my mom, he told her it was because he fell in love. That God finally brought him his soulmate. The only wrong thing about it was the timing.

I think he believed his own lies. He used them as a shield against his sin.

I always believed I was stronger than my dad. I can own my mistakes. I don't need to delude myself to be okay with my actions.

Yet here I am feeling the same pull. Maybe I'm just as vulnerable, seeking justification where there is none. Am I really following my heart, or am I repeating his mistakes, trying to justify my actions and escape the guilt in the same way?

Lily shifts again, and the sheets rustle softly against my skin. "I can't sleep unless you're holding me," she mutters.

My body tenses. "I can't. If I hold you, I'll want more. You need your rest."

She smiles lazily. "A quickie might help me sleep better."

"No." My voice is hoarse with temptation. "You've been tossing and turning all night. You need real sleep now."

She sets her hand on my belly, trailing it downward. "Come on, big guy. Give me that cock."

My need for her ignites within my body like embers flaring to life. With a groan, I roll on top of her. I capture her lips with mine, kissing her with a searing intensity. For all I know, this may be one of my last chances before my sin finally catches up with me.

I'm going to make it count.

As quickly as I can, I free my cock and yank down her panties, not bothering to pull them all the way off. I find her clit so I can ready her for me. Fuck, I need to be inside her soon.

If I could, I would live inside her for the uncertain time we have left. Eventually, God is going to fill my heart with guilt. I don't know why he's taking so long, but I know he's hovering at the edges of my consciousness, waiting to strike.

When I rub her clit in a rapid up-and-down motion, she hums, wiggling her hips. I lower my mouth to her ear. "Good girl. Take what you want from me."

She whimpers as she grinds herself against my hand. Within seconds, a delightful moisture gathers between her thighs. I caress my fingers through it, enjoying the juicy sound it makes.

I position myself at her entrance and look into her eyes. "I'll try to be gentle, sassy girl. I don't want to wear you out."

She places her hand on my cheek. "You don't have to," she rasps. "Your sassy girl likes it rough, even when she's sick."

I push deep inside her, hissing as she clasps around me. Fuck, she's so tight and hot.

Perfect.

"Yes," I growl. "You're my sassy girl. Mine."

"Yours," she says on an exhale, digging her fingers into my shoulders.

Our bodies move in sync, as if we were born joined together. Each thrust is met with a moan. Sweat beads on my forehead as we grind against each other.

The room fills with the sounds of slapping skin and gasps. An overwhelming need consumes my body.

"Tell me you belong to me," I command, trying to quench the ache.

Her eyes are glazed. "I'm yours."

It's not enough.

It could never be enough.

I wrap my arms around her and lift us both to a sitting position. Her pussy clenches around my cock as a distant voice in my head tells me I'm working her too hard. That I should let her rest with her back on the bed while I bring her to completion.

But I need more.

So much more.

I bounce her on my lap, sending a bolt of electricity into my gut.

"Oh God." Her eyes roll back into her head. "That's good."

Her nails dig into my shoulders as I move my hips relentlessly. She starts to contract around my cock, gripping me in her delicious heat.

"Say my name when you come," I demand, thrusting deeper inside her.

"Ethan," she whimpers, and her eyelids flutter closed. She cries out, and I wish I could drink in the sound. Weave it into the fabric of my soul.

A dazzling clarity sparks inside my heart. In my relentless search for God all my life, this is what I was really seeking.

It's always been her.

She's my destiny, my purpose.

The ecstasy explodes within me like fireworks, and I let out a roar. My hands grip her hips, pulling her closer, deeper, harder into me. The world around me sparkles and blurs.

In what feels like an eternity later, she's lying against my chest, her ragged breathing finally growing rhythmic.

"If you're better on Friday," I say, my voice hoarse, "I want you to come to my game."

She swallows. "Yeah?"

"And you're wearing my jersey."

She's quiet for a long while. "You don't care what Noah thinks?"

"No," I say immediately.

And I don't. I'm done hiding. If God has really forsaken me, I have a new dream to fill the longing in my chest.

For now, I'm going to keep it.

I'm going to keep her.

I'll tell Noah everything as soon as I've worked out with Lily what this really means for us. He'll be angry. He might even end our friendship.

It will hurt. It will hurt badly, but I won't give her up for anything.

"Okay," she mutters.

I press my lips against hers, kissing her with a fervent desperation.

I love her. I love her more than I've ever loved anything in my life.

If she's not my true salvation, may God strike me down.

Chapter Twenty-Seven

L ily

Ethan is holding my hand under the restaurant table. It's an innocent touch compared to what he did to me before we left his room today, and yet my belly is on fire.

We're acting like a couple. In public.

Granted, neither my brother nor Brayden—their teammate who is sitting across from us now—have mentioned anything about Ethan and I since we arrived here over an hour ago. I'm not even sure if Noah has noticed the giant number forty-four across my chest.

How dense is my brother?

"Ethan, you're going to seal it tonight," Brayden says. "I'm calling it now. You're getting picked in the first round."

Ethan snorts as he grabs the receipt at the center of the table. He shifts in his seat before pulling out a leather wallet from his back pocket. "Not likely. Even getting picked in the second round would take an act of God." He turns to me with his usual stern expression when I reach for my purse. "I'm paying for you."

I shoot him an innocent frown, mischief sparking within me. "Why would you do that?"

His face stays stoic, but his eyes flash with something that promises retribution later. My tummy flutters at the thought of what it might be. Maybe a harder spanking than last time.

"You're wearing my jersey," he says. "It's customary that I pay for your meal."

"Customary?" I glance around the table. "Is that really true?"

Brayden's eyes grow wide—as if he's uncomfortable—but Noah only shrugs. "Either me or Ethan can pay for you," he says. "We both know what a hardship it is for you to come to a football game. If we pay, we expect you to keep your phone in your pocket and actually watch the game."

I snort. *Either me or Ethan can pay for you,* like they're both my older brothers. Gross. If Noah had even an ounce of intuition, he would notice how sharply Ethan's behavior toward me contrasts with what it was just a few weeks ago.

During our whole lunch, Ethan's eyes haven't strayed from mine. When I couldn't decide between the Western or the jalapeno burger, he ordered both so we could share, claiming they both sounded good—the adorable liar. My big guy even made me drink a full glass of water—damn him—like he's been doing constantly these past few days while I recovered from my fever.

Anyone with eyes could see that Ethan is fucking my brains out behind closed doors, but my brother was never the brightest bulb in the emotional intelligence box.

"No, I'm getting this, Noah," Ethan says, his voice clipped.

He tosses his card onto the bill tray. There's something proprietary about the casual movement, and for the first time, something like recognition sparks in Noah's eyes. His gaze darts between me and Ethan for a moment, his expression thoughtful.

In a flash, the look is gone. "Whatever," Noah says as he grabs his own wallet.

* * *

There's a heaviness in the stadium, and it makes my whole body buzz with anxiety.

Fuck, I wish I understood football better. I know the other team scored, but why has everyone around me grown so gloomy and dejected? The clock says there's still four minutes left. I thought that was a lot in football time.

The girl in front of me twists around, her expression full of anxiety. "I'm dying," she says.

"Me too," I say, but it's a lie. I don't know enough to be dying. What the hell is going on? "I don't really know all the rules, but it seems bad."

She laughs. "That was a crucial third down. We're out of timeouts. They're just going to run the clock down now. We'd need a miracle to turn this around."

I nod, even though her words are gibberish. My gaze flickers to Ethan. I can't see his face with that big helmet covering it, but his body looks defeated.

Poor guy. He hates losing.

The clock ticks down relentlessly. Three minutes. Two minutes. I don't have a clue what's going on, but I know it's bad. Everyone around me is groaning and sighing. Then, with just over a minute left, something happens that makes the crowd cheer and come alive. It seems like the Hawks have a chance again. Ethan takes his position on the field, and my heart pounds in my chest.

You can do this, big guy.

The ball is thrown to Ethan, and he runs like his life depends on it. He jumps to catch it, but a player from the other team crashes into him, and the ball slips from his hands. He falls to the ground, and the crowd around me groans in unison.

The stadium falls into a heavy silence, and my heart jumps into my throat as Ethan slowly gets up from the ground.

At least he isn't hurt.

The clock ticks down to zero, and the game is over. The Hawks lost.

My heart aches for my big guy. I'll have to give him some extra love tonight.

He walks off the field toward the tunnel, and I stand up and grab the railing in front of me. Just as I open my mouth to call out to him, my throat freezes. Mason approaches him on the sidelines. He says something, and Ethan's head snaps in his direction. They exchange words, and Ethan's posture grows stiff and aggressive.

Even from yards away, I feel the fury vibrating from Ethan like heat from the sun. The back of my neck prickles.

Oh God, I think he's about to snap.

Chapter Twenty-Eight

Ethan

The crowd's roar dims to a murmur, and my stomach hollows out. I let everyone down. I see it on all my teammates' faces—the disappointment, the frustration.

I replay in my mind the moment when it all could have been turned around. The ball was perfect, spiraling through the air like a gift from God. It was a rare decent pass from Mason. All I had to do was catch it. But as my fingers touched the ball, the cornerback crashed into me, and the impact knocked the ball loose, along with our chances of winning.

As I walk off the field, Mason catches up to me. Without even looking his way, I can feel his smug smile as if it were scalding me.

"Are you missing your redheaded good luck charm?" he asks. "Oh, wait. I think I saw her in the family section. Wearing your jersey, wasn't she? Maybe she's a redheaded curse."

I grit my teeth and ball my hands into fists. The desire to

punch him is so strong, my hands ache with the need to connect with his face.

He laughs, a grating sound that scrapes against my nerves. "Uh-oh. Don't like me talking bad about her, huh? I'm surprised, Harrington. I never thought a good boy like you would fall for a slut."

I stop in my tracks and turn to face him. An otherworldly aura of rage settles over me, and my periphery blurs, my vision narrowing to Mason's face.

My breathing slows, and the stadium fades, the crowd's noise turning into a distant hum. My heartbeat thumps in my ears.

Mason's face twists in a sneer, his eyes glinting with malice. My fists tighten, and the desire to make him feel even a fraction of the pain he's caused Lily becomes the call of my soul.

My fist flies through the air, driven by a force I can't control. It connects with his face in a satisfying crunch, and the impact reverberates up my arm. Mason stumbles back, clutching his nose and crumpling to the ground.

The stadium erupts around us, a roar of gasps and shouts. A primal satisfaction courses through me. I stand over him, watching him writhe on the ground.

Coach Rodriguez is yelling, his voice sharp and angry, but it sounds like it's coming from a great distance, muffled compared to the roaring in my head.

I can't tear my eyes away from Mason. Seeing him in pain and knowing I caused it brings a twisted sense of vindication.

"That was for Lily," I say.

With a satisfied smile, I glance up into the stands, my gaze searching for my sassy girl. I hope she saw this. I hope she had the satisfaction of watching Mason crumple over like a card tower.

Then I find her. She's standing by the railing at the front of the family section. Her body is utterly still. Even from yards away, I can make out the expression on her face.

Shocked. Lifeless. Like she's just seen something terrible.

Because she didn't want me to lay a finger on Mason, and

somehow, in my haze of rage, I completely forgot about the promise I gave her.

Fuck, I'll have to apologize.

Only for breaking that promise, though. Not for punching Mason. After the provocation he gave me, no power on heaven or earth could have stopped me from finally taking him down.

"My office," Coach Rodriguez shouts, making me jump. "Now, Harrington."

I wince before looking up into the stands. Lily's eyes lock with mine. "I'm sorry," I mouth.

Her eyes grow cold, and her lips wobble. She shakes her head before turning around and walking up the bleacher steps.

A jolt of panic shoots through me, but I try to squash it. It won't help to be distracted while Coach Rodriguez rips into me.

Everything will be okay with Lily. She'll forgive me once she sees that I had no other choice. Letting Mason get away with calling her a slut after what he did to her would have been the death of my goddamn soul.

Chapter Twenty-Nine

L ily

I pace back and forth outside the locker room, heat rising to my cheeks. Each step I take only seems to stoke the fire of my anger more.

Without thinking, Ethan dragged the worst moment of my life into the public eye. Mason won't keep his mouth shut after this. He'll jump on the defensive, fearing that I might come forward about the rape. He might even invent stories to preemptively discredit me.

She's crazy. She wanted me, and I rejected her. Now she's getting revenge. Isn't that what dipshit men usually say about women who accuse them of rape?

And thanks to Ethan's recent fame, it might not only be the campus talking about my shame. There's a good chance that punch on the field will make national news.

The whole world could find out what happened to me. I'll be forever branded as a broken woman, assuming I'm even believed.

Rage grips my chest, making it hard to breathe. Ethan had better not try to tell me that punch was for my sake. It was all about him and his righteous indignation. He wanted to take justice into his own hands, to make Mason pay.

He didn't even think about how it would affect me. How my life could unravel as a result.

When my eyes grow misty, I inhale a shaky breath. No tears now. I need to end this with Ethan first.

When I glance at my watch, anxiety prickles my skin. It's a welcome distraction from my anger. Ethan's been in the locker room a long time, when almost every other player has left. The only people who haven't come through that door are Mason, Noah, and Ethan.

My stomach churns. If Ethan's been in there this long, he's probably in serious trouble.

And Mason is most likely being treated by the medics. That punch sent him flying. His nose is probably broken.

The memory of him crumpling to the ground is the only joy to be taken from this mess. Even in my inner turmoil, it was satisfying to see him finally feel some form of suffering on my behalf.

But the satisfaction was short-lived. Mason's nose will heal, but what will this all mean for me? Oh God, what's going to happen?

What if I'm judged for that wretched night—the darkest moment of my life—and found lacking? I can already hear people discussing the details.

Why did she get so drunk? She let him sleep in her bed. That doesn't sound like rape to me.

Fuck, I can't think about this. It's too much. I'll go crazy.

The locker room door finally swings open, and Ethan steps out. Relief washes through my veins. His stride is far too confident for someone who was either suspended or kicked off the team.

When my gaze lifts to his face, my relief is washed out as if by a deluge.

His expression is defiant—jaw set and eyes burning. He doesn't even care that he just dropped a bomb on my life. In fact, he looks smug about it.

I stride up to him, lifting my chin. "What was that about?"

Ethan meets my gaze unflinchingly. "He deserved it."

"It doesn't matter what he deserved," I snap. "I told you not to do this. I told you not to fight my battles for me."

He opens his mouth to argue, but I hold up a hand. "You don't get it. You think you're protecting me, but all you're doing is making things worse."

He clenches his jaw. "I couldn't just stand by and do nothing. I've been pushed—" His voice cracks, and he inhales a shaky breath. "I've reached my limit. I've stayed quiet about this for too long. Mason provoked me tonight. I'm not going to repeat what he said about you, but trust me when I tell you, he deserved what he got."

"What he said about me?" I scoff. "He's a rapist, Ethan. Who the fuck cares what he has to say about anything?"

A storm of fury builds behind Ethan's dark-blue eyes. "He called you a name." He shakes his head. "I won't even tell you what it is."

I groan. "So he called me a whore?"

The flaring of his nostrils is the only answer I need. My groan is so hoarse it's almost a growl. "I don't care if he called me a whore. He's trash. A slimy little worm. All I want is to forget him. How do you not realize what you've done? He's never going to leave me alone after this."

Ethan crosses his arms over his chest. "He won't ever come near you again. I'll kill him if he does."

"Oh. My. God." I place both hands on my burning cheeks. "Do you hear yourself? You're making this all about you."

His expression softens. "I'm not, Lily." He reaches out his hand and strokes my hair. "You've been suffering alone, and it kills me. You don't have to. You have people... People who love you. Let them take the burden, if only for a while. I can deal with

Mason, not because you aren't capable of doing it, but because you shouldn't have to."

His words warm me against my better judgment. I have people who love me, he said. Not him. Just people in general.

A tear falls down my cheek, but I quickly wipe it away. "It doesn't matter. You promised that you would let me handle this. I thought your promises meant something."

His expression grows pained. "Yes, I broke a promise, but there wasn't another option, sassy girl. I couldn't stand there and let him say ugly things about you. Not after what he did."

His use of my nickname usually makes my stomach flutter, but not in this moment. He's saying it to coddle me. I'm acting like an overly emotional woman, in his eyes. Too worked up to know what's good for me.

I take a step back, and Ethan's hand falls to his side. He looks bewildered, hurt, but I can't let him get off easily. I need a man who sees me as an equal, who respects my wishes even when he doesn't agree with them.

"You don't care about me," I say. "This was all about you."

As soon as the words are out, I want to suck them back in. Ethan flinches as if I struck him, his face growing pale.

It wasn't fair to say that. He's one of the most caring people I know. But why couldn't he keep his promise? I've come to rely on his steadiness, his predictability.

Ethan's eyes darken, the hurt quickly transforming into anger. "How dare you say I don't care about you." The words are quiet. "Yes, I broke a promise, and I would do it again. I defend the people I care about, because that's who I am. If you can't handle it, then this thing between us won't work."

A sharp pain cuts into my chest, and a burning sensation blooms behind my eyes.

How like Ethan to draw a line in the sand, to present an ultimatum. He's forcing me to choose. It's his way or the highway.

I lift my chin, meeting his gaze. "If that's how you see it, then maybe you're right. Maybe this won't work."

Ethan's face crumples. His eyes search mine desperately, like a drowning man reaching out for a lifeline. His lips part, but no words come out.

The silence stretches, heavy and suffocating.

My heart cracks in my chest, splitting in two. One part of me screams to wrap my arms around him, to say I forgive him. But the other part—the part that's grown stronger over these last few weeks—refuses to waver. I won't be pushed into a corner. I'll never let a man force me to do anything ever again.

I swallow hard, forcing back the tears that threaten to spill. "Goodbye, Ethan."

I turn and walk away. As I leave him behind, the tears finally break free and stream down my face. My chest tightens, the ache of leaving him nearly unbearable. But I keep moving, determined to find my own strength, even if it means walking away from the man I love.

I do love him. It's only now that he's forced my hand that I see it. This wonderful man treats me like a precious jewel, but he also wants to guard me like a dragon. Use his strict morality as an excuse to lock me in a box.

I won't allow it, even though my heart is shattering. I refuse to be caged, however sweet his care and coddling might be. I'm on the path to reclaiming the wild and free girl I once was, and damn it, I won't let anyone get in the way.

Chapter Thirty

E than

Her retreating form grows gradually smaller, each step taking her farther away from me. Why does it look like the whole world is leaching of color, dimming dull gray?

Panic grips my chest. I want to call out to her, to make her stop, but the words stick in my throat.

She made a choice. She doesn't want me. Not the real me, at least. I've already given up so much. I've even grown to accept that God has abandoned me. But I refuse to give up my soul for her.

This dim, colorless world is hell, but it's nothing new, is it? This is the existence I knew before her. All monotonous routine.

When she came into my world, she lit the whole thing up. Her presence was a flame, bringing light and heat to the darkest corners of my life. Now, the fire is dying, the cold seeping back in. I want to escape it. To capture her fire and keep it with me forever.

But how can I back down? I meant it when I said that this is who I am. I can't let injustice go unpunished. I can't undergo a personality transplant just to make her happy.

Is this you, God? Are you finally speaking to me, punishing me for my sins? If you are, you've gone too far. It feels as if the very essence of me is unraveling, thread by thread.

Footsteps echo on the concrete, and I look up to see Noah coming around the corner of the building.

"What the fuck was that?" His voice is low and controlled, but his eyes are full of fury.

He must have heard that whole conversation.

I swallow hard. My throat is so dry. "There's a lot…" I shut my eyes. "A lot I haven't told you."

He huffs out a humorless laugh. "Yeah, it sounds like it." He takes a step closer, his eyes growing wide. "What did Lily mean?"

I flinch at the sharpness in his tone. "About what?"

"Don't give me that. What did she mean about Mason? She called him a rapist."

I rub my hand over my damp forehead. "You'll have to talk to her. It's not my story to tell."

He crosses his arms over his chest. "You'd better fucking tell me now. Or else our friendship is over."

Pain shoots into my chest, but it barely registers. The feeling is only a dull throb. After losing Lily, I'm like a ghost. The world around me continues to move, but I'm disconnected.

"That's your choice." My voice is as lifeless as I feel. "I can't betray Lily."

He scoffs. "I can't believe you. I don't even know who you are. What did that mean when you said this thing between you wasn't going to work. Were you in some kind of relationship with her behind my back?

I let out a heavy sigh. "Yes."

He scowls. "How serious was it?"

I swallow. "Serious. Well, I should say…it was serious for me."

Noah's mouth drops open, his shock so palpable I could reach out and touch it. "Oh fuck." He sets both hands on the top of his head. "Oh, holy fuck. You lost your virginity to her, huh?"

I can only nod.

He doesn't respond. Instead, he turns away and starts pacing the concrete in front of me. "Oh, shit." He halts and looks at me for a moment but then starts pacing again. "So many lies. I can't... I seriously don't even know you."

I shut my eyes. "I'm sorry."

His footsteps halt. When I open my eyes, he's glaring daggers at me. "Sorry isn't enough. You've been lying to me. You. The most trustworthy person I know. I can't believe this." His expression shifts from anger to disbelief. "She was raped, and you didn't tell me... You lost your virginity to her... I didn't even have a clue." As if a thought occurs to him, his face hardens. "You punched Mason tonight for her, huh? Because you knew what he did to her."

When I don't respond, he clenches his hands into fists. "Answer the question."

I raise my chin, refusing to let him guilt me into a confession that isn't mine to give. "I told you. Ask her."

"She's my fucking sister, Ethan," he shouts. "I'm the one who's supposed to take care of her. Fuck, I've been living with Mason. The man who raped my sister." He shakes his head, his eyes growing unfocused. "I could have smothered that motherfucker in his sleep." His gaze snaps to my face. "Why didn't she tell me?"

I inhale an unsteady breath. "It's not my place to tell you her secrets."

"Secrets." Noah releases a long, measured breath. "So many secrets. I feel like we were never friends."

When my throat grows tight, I cough to clear it. "You're the best friend I've ever had."

His eyes flash. "Well, you're not mine. Not if you could lie to me like this." He shakes his head. "I thought you were the best guy I knew. If I thought you had any interest in her, I might have…" His jaw hardens. "But now I know you're a fucking liar. All your morals and Bible thumping. It's just a cover, huh? You preach about doing the right thing, but when it comes down to it, you're just a lying dirtbag. You probably kept Lily's secret from me just because you wanted to please her. Just so you could get her into bed with you."

A spark of anger ignites within me, injecting a surge of energy into my lifeless body. "No. I love her."

He scoffs. "I don't believe it." He takes a step back, the disdain clear in his eyes. "You're saying that to try to make up for all your lies." With that, he turns on his heel and marches away, leaving me standing alone in the dark.

I just lost my best friend in the world. Why is there only a faint throb in my chest? Probably because I lost the ability to feel when Lily said goodbye.

What is one more wave crashing over me when I'm already drowning?

L ily

Me: I can't stay with a man who doesn't respect my wishes.

My fingers tremble as I hit send, and a hollow ache settles in my chest. Packing up my things in Ethan's room doesn't take long, and yet it's grueling.

His room became my haven, but I don't belong here anymore. He made his choice tonight. Apparently, his principles are more important than my feelings.

As I step out into the hallway, my chest tightens. I don't want to go back to my sorority house, even though I love my girls.

I love Ethan more. It's excruciating that he couldn't choose me.

When I open the door to my sorority house, Kinsley is sitting on the living room couch.

"Lily." She jumps from her seat and walks toward me. "What's going on? Is your week with Ethan up already?"

Her voice is so gentle, so motherly, that the facade I've been holding on to crumbles. My eyes grow misty.

"I had to leave," I say. "I couldn't stay anymore."

Her eyes grow wide. "There was more to it than just him helping you out, wasn't there?"

A lump forms in my throat, and I can only nod. Kinsley seems to understand immediately, because she nearly leaps on me. "I knew he was in love with you. I knew it all along. Oh, honey. What did he do?"

I lean into her warmth. "He can't accept me as I am," I say in a choked voice. "He wants to stick to his strict Ethan code regardless of how it affects me. It's more important to him than a promise he made to me."

She squeezes me tightly before letting me go and looking into my eyes. "He's a stubborn guy. That's for sure. But, Lily, I really think he's one of the good ones. Maybe he just needs a little more time."

"No," I say firmly. "Something happened tonight. He..." I wince. None of this is going to make sense to her since I never told her the full truth. Oh well, I'll tell her what I can. "He punched Mason because of me. On the sidelines after the game tonight. You might even see it on the news."

She pulls away, her eyes growing huge. "He punched him? Because...Mason is your ex?"

I lower my gaze to the carpet beneath my feet. "It's a complicated story, and I'll tell you all of it when I'm ready."

She nods slowly. "I always thought there was more to your breakup than you let on."

My throat grows tight. "There was."

Her expression softens. "Well, I'm here whenever you need me."

I let out a heavy breath. For the first time in months, the idea of telling another person about what happened to me doesn't fill me with shame. I can thank Ethan for that.

Maybe it's a good thing that Ethan and I were thrown together, even if it ultimately broke my heart. He taught me I can't stay bottled up forever, that all it does is make the pressure of my troubles build like bubbles in a shaken champagne bottle, ready to explode at any moment.

I might finally be able to sleep in my own dreaded bedroom tonight, but it's little consolation.

I'll miss those big arms wrapped around me, and the steady comfort of his heartbeat. But I'm strong enough to prioritize needs.

I just wish I didn't have to.

* * *

Ethan

Her things are gone.

It doesn't take a detailed search to confirm it. The few items she'd brought with her—her duffel bag, the toothbrush sitting on my sink, the clothes she left strewn on the floor after the last time I peeled them off—are nowhere to be found.

I already knew she wouldn't be here. Her text implied she'd be gone.

Yet a chilling emptiness spreads through me, and memories of the day my dad left come flooding through my mind. All his things were gone too.

When I cried and told my mom he left because I was bad—the silly fear of a child—she held me and told me it had nothing to do with me. That moms and dads get in fights. That he would be coming back.

It was months before she learned the full extent of what he did, and even when she tried to shield the details from me, I knew.

She couldn't hide that there was someone else. Not when I had to stay with my dad's mistress during my rare weekends with him.

I knew the truth. He chose that woman over us. Because what we provided him wasn't fulfilling enough for his insatiable, selfish quest for what he called happiness.

Over time, I got over it. I decided I was lucky that blustering prick moved out. Lucky that he cared so little about me that he rarely exercised his custody rights. Hell, he paid my mom more child support just to avoid me.

This loss feels different. In this moment, this ache in my heart feels permanent, a scar that will follow me everywhere, even into death.

Lily brought into my life something I never knew existed: pure, unbridled joy. She's become my key to unlocking the beauty and tenderness that life can offer. Without her, I'm lost in a sea of unquenchable longing. A void not even God can fill.

Just like I was before she came into my life.

Despair wraps around me like a vise, squeezing tighter with each second. I sink onto the edge of the bed, burying my face in my hands.

The room is cold, lifeless without her. The light in my heart has been shut off, leaving me in darkness.

Chapter Thirty-Two

E than

I dreamed about Lily last night. She had a fever, but this time, she was so sick that Dr. Carter came to my room to see her. After one look at her lying listlessly on my bed, he told me she wasn't going to make it.

I started screaming at him, demanding that he do more. I listed a slew of medical procedures he needed to try before he gave up, because apparently, I'm an overbearing control freak even in my sleep. He wouldn't listen. He left the room, and a profound powerlessness settled over me.

Some things can't be fixed. The world is full of suffering. It's inevitable, even when you stand by your principles and strive to make the right choices.

I crouched down by my bed next to my sassy girl. She was lifeless, barely moving. I gripped her hand, wanting to beg her to stay, to tell her I'd be nothing without her. My life would lose its meaning.

I couldn't speak. My voice was frozen.

The last thing I remember is stroking her red hair with the haunting certainty that I'd never see it again.

When I woke up, my eyes were wet.

Dreams are bizarre. Lily isn't dead. Her vibrant spirit will continue to light up the world.

But not mine. I'll be a footnote in her story, a brief disappointment. Boring, predictable Ethan Harrington who chose himself over her wishes.

"Are you listening, Ethan?" Coach Rodriguez asks.

I let out a heavy sigh. He just told me the university administration has decided to keep me on the team without disciplinary action. I ought to be ecstatic, and here I am, ruminating about death and suffering. When did football drop so low on my list of priorities?

Probably around the time Lily started staying with me.

"Yeah," I say. "I'm really...lucky."

He leans forward, placing his elbows on his desk. "This doesn't mean anything about your draft prospects, so don't think you got off scot-free. Your behavior on the field, your character... It all matters. GMs will think twice about drafting a loose cannon who might punch the quarterback after a bad game. It's all over the damn news. I'm sure you've seen it."

"I have," I say, but it's a lie. The only way I know that me punching Mason has been replayed on sports news shows is from texts I've gotten from teammates.

Coach is quiet for a long while, examining my face with narrowed eyes. "It doesn't add up. I know your character. That wasn't like you. You're not the type of player to punch a teammate because he threw a bad pass."

I laugh humorlessly. "It was actually a pretty decent pass for Mason."

"Stop," Coach says sharply. "I think you're brushing this off because you're trying to avoid telling me what happened. What did he say to you out there?"

"I never thought a good boy like you would fall for a slut."

I blink hard to clear the memory. "He said something...really ugly about a girl I like." When my throat grows tight, I swallow hard. "A girl I love."

Coach nods slowly, as if expecting me to say more.

I stay silent, staring at the wooden desk. Was punching Mason the right thing to do? I'm not even sure anymore. Nothing feels right now that Lily is gone.

All I know is that nothing could have stopped me from throwing that punch. Even after everything he did to her, he called her that ugly word. Like she's nothing. Like she's trash. The truth is that *he's* trash, and she's as radiant and essential as the sun.

Coach crosses his arms over his chest. "Well, it's not over, so don't start slacking off. The Redwood State game on Saturday could save you. Your performance against them last year sealed your draft prospects. You're too talented to ignore."

"Yeah, maybe."

His jaw clenches. "You need to think hard about your future. This won't be the only time you face provocation on the field. People will say things to get under your skin, to make you lose control. You have to be better than that. You have to rise above it."

I nod slightly, but I still say nothing. It's impossible to pretend like I care about football right now.

The shrill ring of my phone cuts through the tension. I glance down and see Kinsley's name lighting up the screen. What the fuck? I didn't even realize I had her number programmed in my phone. "I need to take this."

Coach nods. "Go ahead."

I swipe the screen and bring the phone to my ear. "What's up, Kinsley?"

"Is Lily with you?" Her tone is urgent, and my heart hitches, beginning to pound against my chest.

"No." My voice is strained. "What's going on?"

"She told Lorelai she was going for a hike on Inspiration Point. She was supposed to be back hours ago. I'm sure she's fine, but it's dark now, and we're all worried. I've been trying her phone, and it just goes straight to voicemail."

A cold wave washes over me, my pulse throbbing in my ears. I leap up from the chair. "I'll go look for her. Are you sure she said Inspiration Point?"

"Positive. Do you want me to come with you?"

"No. I'll go alone."

She'll only slow me down. She doesn't have the stamina to run to the top of Inspiration Point.

Or the motivation.

After I hang up, my gaze snaps to Coach. His expression is a mixture of concern and confusion. "The girl I mentioned... She's missing. I'm sorry to cut our meeting short."

He stands up from his chair. "Go," he says, and I dart toward the door, halting at the sound of Coach's voice. "Ethan."

I turn around, my body itching to get out of this room. "Yeah?"

"Try to resolve your personal struggles before Saturday. Your head needs to be in the game."

I nod once. "Absolutely."

Except the truth is I don't even care. I need to find Lily, so I run from his office as if a fire is chasing me.

Chapter Thirty-Three

L ily

Sometimes I wish I had a god. Sure, I don't like being told what to do or having my freedom restrained. But a little advice—gently given, of course, no tyrannical deities for me—would be nice right now.

Ethan is so certain about right and wrong. I don't think he even has to ask for advice. An inner voice is always guiding him, making him confident in all his decisions.

"He deserved what he got."

Ethan was so certain about it, like that punch in the face was sanctioned by the divine.

Outside of the incident on the field yesterday, I've grown to love his convictions. He's trustworthy, dependable, like a boulder in a river.

In my life, *I'm* the river. Flowing ceaselessly and splitting in different directions. Fun and freedom are my guiding light, and I run away at the first sight of pain. I'm not even sure if I believe in right and wrong.

Was I selfish for making Ethan promise not to take action against Mason? Yesterday, he'd seemed ravaged by the burden of what I'd told him, which I'd somehow never noticed before.

It makes sense given his character. The weight of his own principles must have been pressing down on him, fighting with his promise to stand by my wishes.

I hate the thought of my big guy being troubled, having to shoulder the consequences of my decisions. I thought I was standing up for my needs, but was it worth it if I made Ethan compromise himself?

I love him, just as he is—my darling control freak who always considers my needs. Who takes care of me when I refuse to take care of myself.

What would happen if I gave in to his moral code for the chance to have that blissful happiness with him? Would he use that to restrict my freedom?

I'm startled by a distant sound. A rustling of some kind.

Shit. When did it get dark? I've been sitting on this boulder for who knows how long as I process the events of yesterday. I can barely see the ocean. There's just a sliver of moonlight sparkling near the horizon.

A moment later, frantic footsteps pound against a rocky path. A rush of adrenaline prickles my skin. A beam of light slices through the darkness. I recoil, pressing myself against the cold stone at my back to hide.

"Lily, is that you?" Ethan's hoarse voice cuts through the night, and I let out the breath I was holding.

His body emerges from the shadows, his silhouette framed by the flashlight's glare. As he steps closer, the light falls away, and I switch on my phone's flashlight to see him better. His chest rises and falls rapidly, his shirt clinging to his torso. What the hell is he doing here, and why is he soaking wet?

"Did you go swimming or something?" I ask.

"Swimming?" Ethan's voice is a sharp bark. "No, I didn't go swimming, Lily." His breath comes in ragged gasps. "I'm soaked in sweat because I've been running uphill for forty-five damn minutes straight trying to find you."

His eyes burn with an intensity that makes my heart stutter.

He throws up his hands. "What are you doing up here in the dark? Alone? It's not safe. You should never hike alone at night, Lily. Never."

Anger flares suddenly. Here I was softening toward him, and he's come to remind me that he's a tyrant.

"I came up here to clear my head," I say. "A lot happened yesterday. Do I need to refresh your memory?"

His stern expression falters for a moment, but the fire quickly reignites behind his eyes. "I'm not the only one worried. Kinsley called me. Your whole house was expecting you back by now. They've been trying to call you for hours."

Guilt edges into my anger. "I don't think there's any reception up here," I mutter.

He runs his fingers through the wet hair matted to his head, his hand shaking. "I've been losing my fucking mind. Using this goddamn flashlight to check the ravines in case you'd fallen. I don't think I've ever been—" His lips close. He sets a hand on his chest as he takes a deep breath. "I've ever been so scared in my life."

As he stands there panting, I finally take in his appearance. His disheveled hair is plastered to his forehead, and his cheeks are bright red. Beneath the flush, his face is drawn and there are dark circles under his eyes.

"I'm sorry I made you worry," I say. "But really, Ethan, this is getting old. You don't seem to trust me to protect myself. I'd think after everything that happened yesterday, you'd have learned…"

I can't say any more, because I don't even know my own heart. I'm warmed that he still cares this much for me after my condemnation of him yesterday, but I don't know what to do.

Could I be in a relationship with someone who draws such hard lines between right and wrong? Someone who's so overbearingly protective that he makes decisions for me without considering my feelings?

Plus, I don't even know if he wants a relationship with me. We've never really talked about it. The brief fling we had was like a haven. We were in a private world of just the two of us.

"I don't have the right to care about you?" Ethan spits out. "No, I guess not. I've been banished for being myself and standing up for what I thought was right. You left me!"

I flinch at his words. The pain in his face is almost unbearable to see.

Ethan grimaces. "I came home, and all of your things were gone. It was hell, Lily. Worse than—"

When he shuts his eyes, bewilderment expands like a balloon within me. "Worse than what?" Oh no. Guilt sinks my gut like a stone. How could I have forgotten that his dad left him and his mom so suddenly? How he'd been the most vulnerable I'd ever seen him when he told me that story. "Like when your dad left."

He inhales a shaky breath. "My mom and I came home from an away game one weekend, and..." He shakes his head. "You can probably guess the rest."

I didn't think at all. I was making a statement. *This is what happens when you cross me, Ethan Harrington.*

It was thoughtless and selfish.

"I'm sorry, Ethan." My voice barely carries over the breeze that has picked up and is rustling the leaves around us. "I didn't think..." I shut my eyes, straining to find the words. "I left your house because I was pissed off. That was as far as I thought. I wasn't trying to hurt you, but I felt so... I still feel so... betrayed."

Ethan grunts, shaking his head. "Strange that someone standing up for you would make you feel betrayed, especially when you don't seem to have any desire to stand up for yourself."

Anger flares suddenly, dampening my sympathy. How dare he

call me out because my beliefs don't happen to match his. The truth is he broke a promise to me, and he still won't own up to it.

He's rigid and stubborn. He would walk all over me if I let him.

I push myself off the boulder and march in his direction, stopping inches away from his chest. His musky scent washes over me, reminding me of his crazy sprint up the trail. My God, he really is soaked from head to toe in sweat. I'd probably laugh if I weren't ready to bite his head off.

"I do stand up for myself," I say. "And my own needs, which you completely ignored when you punched Mason. I don't need to prove anything to you. I never claimed to have my shit together."

His eyes narrow. "What if there are others, Lily?"

I frown. "What do you mean, others?"

"What if you're not the only woman Mason's hurt? Hell, think about the women he might hurt in the future. Would you be willing to stand up for them?"

His words hit me like a slap. Dizziness descends over me, causing the world around me to spin and distort.

Other women.

Why have I never thought of that before? My stomach churns at the thought of them—maybe a freshman, young and scared, caught in the same nightmare. An eighteen-year-old version of me flashes in my mind. How would she have handled it?

She didn't know herself yet. Going to parties and getting drunk were her way of adjusting to the overwhelming new world around her. If someone had hurt her deeply, she would have been lost.

Is there a girl like her out there somewhere on campus that feels alone and vulnerable? I see her lying in bed, staring at the ceiling, unable to sleep. Every small noise in the hallway makes her jump. She's wondering if this is the new normal, if she'll live the rest of her life in fear, exhaustion, and bone-deep loneliness.

I'm going to be sick.

"Lily." Ethan's voice is a caress. He reaches out and strokes my cheek with his fingers. "My sweet, sassy girl. It wouldn't be your fault. I didn't mean that."

My eyes mist over, and I take a steadying breath. "I want to go home."

He stares at me for a moment before nodding. "Let's go."

Chapter Thirty-Four

E than

I grip the steering wheel so tightly my knuckles turn white, the muscles in my forearms straining. My gaze darts in Lily's direction. She's as still and quiet as the dead. It's so unlike her, and it's all my fault. With careless words, I tossed a heavy burden on her shoulders that doesn't belong there.

I never should have brought up the possibility of Mason hurting other women. She's not responsible for him doing anything to anyone else. Quite the opposite. It's people like me—unharmed by the perpetrator—who need to take a stand.

As we pull up in front of the sorority house, my throat tightens. I swallow hard and turn to her, and my heart sinks. She looks so small, so fragile. The need to reach out and touch her, to offer comfort, is overwhelming.

I don't have the right, and it's a physical pain in my chest.

Who cares about standing up for what you believe in? If it means losing the woman I love, what is it even worth?

"I'm sorry," I say, my voice barely above a whisper. "I'm sorry for what I said. You don't have to think about anyone but yourself. It's not your responsibility to take care of Mason's victims, assuming there even are more. That's on us. The people who..." I swallow. "The people who love you."

Life sparks in her eyes, and my heart starts to pound. I sit for what feels like an eternity waiting for her to respond.

"You're such a good person," she finally says, and my stomach plummets.

Not the response I was hoping for, but then again, it was a rather weak confession of love. In fact, it sounded almost familial. Like she's just one of the many people I love. Not the heartbeat that keeps me alive.

"I'm not a good person," I say. "I'm just a try-hard. Inside, I'm weak. I know what's right, but it takes all my willpower to do it. I've realized that because of you. The reason I'm so... fucking uptight is because I'm not good on my own. Unlike you." Unable to help myself, I reach out and stroke the fine strands of hair around her temple. "You're good all on your own."

She snorts. "I didn't take you for a bullshitter, but then again, you've probably decided that making me feel better for being such a self-absorbed asshole is worth telling a lie. What good do I actually do? I have no principles."

I shut my eyes, remorse washing over me. "What good do you do? People like me would live a joyless existence without fire-crackers like you. You bring good to the world just by being yourself. Your energy, your passion, it lifts everyone around you, especially me. You make the world more vibrant, more alive."

"That's really sweet, Ethan." Her voice is small, choked.

If she starts crying, I won't be able to contain myself. I'll have to take her in my arms. Hell, I might even carry her into my house and up to my room. Our room. Where she belongs.

She turns to me, and those stormy-gray eyes are full of pain, but there are no tears, which is somehow even worse. "What good is any of that if I'm selfish?" She shakes her head. "You were right. By staying silent, I could potentially hurt other people."

I flinch. "No. I already told you, it's not on you to—"

"Who else could do it?" She raises her voice. "Who else could make Mason face consequences but a person he hurt?" Her lips quiver, and her gaze falls to her lap. "I hurt you too. The most wonderful man I know."

"Lily." Her name is a plea on my lips.

She turns to me and sets her hand on my cheek, and I lean into the touch. "We'll talk soon. I have to fix this first. I'm determined."

"What do you mean—"

My heart jumps into my throat when her hand slips away and she opens the car door. I want to shout at her to come back. To tell her I love her and beg her to never leave me.

She shuts the door, and the chance is gone.

In a frenzy, I yank out my phone and pull up Brandon's name. I need my brother right now. Someone who knows me. Who can anchor me.

* * *

I follow Brandon out of the kitchen and onto the balcony. Under the dim glow of the patio lights, he strides over to the outdoor fridge. He pulls out a beer, pops the lid, and promptly sits at the glass table beside me.

"You look like hell," he says.

I snort. "Yeah, I don't know if you heard, but I punched my own quarterback yesterday. In front of an entire stadium."

Sarcasm, of course. He and my sister-in-law, Mariana, were in that stadium. He's been calling me nonstop since it happened.

Brandon's mouth grows tense, as if he's fighting a smile. "The first thing Mari said when it happened was that the dude deserved it. She said she doesn't know what he said to you, but she knows he deserved it."

I huff. "He did, but it might have cost me my whole career. I made myself look like a deranged menace in front of scouts. What team wants to take on a liability like that?"

Brandon's eyes narrow. "Tell me if I'm wrong, but I get the impression that you're not as upset about what the scouts saw as you're letting on. In fact, I don't think that's why you wanted to see me tonight. I think you want to talk about the girl who has driven you crazy for years."

Brandon's gaze is piercing, and I struggle to keep my expression neutral. He knows me well, but I wasn't expecting him to get to the heart of my troubles so quickly.

I run my fingers through my hair and grip it tightly, sending tingles into my scalp. "I love her. I also... I lost my virginity to her."

"I thought that might happen," he says immediately, making me jerk back in my seat.

"You did?" I ask, incredulity making my head fuzzy. "You must know me a lot better than I know myself. I thought for sure I would save myself for my future wife. In fact, I thought that up until the moment I made the impulsive decision to have sex with Lily. The worst part is, I don't feel any guilt. I'd do it all over again if I had the chance."

"Ethan..." He shakes his head. "You know my thoughts on purity culture and how toxic it is, so I won't preach to you about it. But it never seemed to me that your plan to stay a virgin until marriage held much conviction. It was like an item on one of your many internal checklists. Your proof to yourself that you have morals and discipline. That you're a good person."

Irritation sends prickles of heat over my skin. "What are principles if not a framework to live by? They're my way of making sure I'm doing right by others and by myself. They're not just a checklist, they're my guideposts. Without them, I'd be lost."

He reaches out and sets a hand on my shoulder. "You wouldn't be. You're stronger than you think. Principles are important, but they shouldn't be a cage. Life is messy, and sometimes you have to bend a little. It doesn't mean you're lost. It means you're human. I don't know where you got the idea that you have to be perfect to be good."

I scoff. "I don't think I have to be perfect."

"Then why do you beat yourself up over every little mistake? The way you just talked about losing your virginity..." He shakes his head. "You told me you love that girl. Why should you feel guilty for having sex with her?"

I let out a long sigh. "I made a vow to God that I would save myself for my wife, and at my first real temptation, I threw that vow out the window. I've barely thought about God at all since Lily came into my life. I haven't even gone to church. She's all I think about. I'm obsessed with her."

His smile is almost pitying. "Love does that, and it's a beautiful thing. God can handle it. He doesn't need your constant attention. And maybe you don't care about your faith right now because it hasn't been kind to you. It's too rigid. Too restraining. Maybe God is trying to tell you that you need to redefine your faith."

"What does that even mean?"

Brandon leans closer, his dark eyes burning into mine. "It means faith isn't a straitjacket. A god that demands a miserable existence of you isn't a god at all."

"Well, it's the only God I've ever known. You're one of his shepherds. Maybe have a talk with him about my miserable existence. See if he can do something about it."

"I don't think we have the same God. Mine isn't as judgmental as yours. Mine brings me happiness and clarity."

A tingling sensation spread through my body. It's like I've been jolted awake from a long, restless sleep.

"Oh, fuck," I mutter.

No wonder I became so obsessed with Lily. She brought something into my life that I never truly knew before. Blissful, aching joy. With her, I was free for the first time, unburdened by the heavy weight of my self-imposed expectations. I spent so many years trying hard to be perfect, to be nothing like my father. I used this idea of a rigid God and his rules to help me feel like I was righteous and deserving, but I was never happy.

I'm not sure if I even know the real God. It doesn't matter if my old faith crumbles away. What matters is finding something real, something that brings me life and joy.

Right now, the only thing that feels real and true is *her*.

The real God can find me in his own time. For now, I'm going to work on gaining back the trust of the one girl who showed me what it means to live.

My darling, precious Lily.

I only hope it's not too late.

"Brandon," I say, my pulse pounding in my ears. "I fucked up. I betrayed Lily."

His eyes widen. "Betrayed her how?"

I wave a hand. "It's a long story, and it's not my place to tell you the details. But that punch yesterday had nothing to do with the game. I punched Mason because I wanted to punish him, even after Lily made me promise I would stay out of it. The worst part is...I wouldn't listen." I shake my head, my thoughts growing fuzzy. "I acted like it was my moral obligation to punch him in the face."

He laughs, a deep, hearty sound that resonates through the cool night air. "Moral obligation to punch him in the face. Oh, Ethan."

My face heats. "It sounds fucking stupid after saying it aloud."

"It sounds like you're in love, and you wanted to protect your woman."

I wince. "I shouldn't have done it. Not when she made me promise. Her feelings should be so much more important than my need to avenge her. I think... It came from a dark place. Possessiveness. I want to protect her, to keep her safe from everything that could hurt her. But more than that, I want it to be my exclusive right. I want to be the center of her world, like she is mine."

Brandon takes a slow sip of his beer. When he sets it down on the table, he stares at me for a long moment. "There's nothing wrong with wanting to protect her, as long as you respect her autonomy. You can learn how to do that. We're all a work in progress. Let this be your first lesson that you don't have to be perfect."

He's right. I can grow and change, unlearn my rigid habits.

But the first thing I need to do is show Lily that I'm willing. That I'm ready to throw my idol of perfection and moral superiority into the fire.

I need to prove to her that I can be the man she needs—the man who respects her choices and stands by her side, no matter what. I want to be the partner she can lean on, not the hero who tries to solve everything for her.

I take a deep breath, a sense of determination raging like a fire within me. I can fix this. It's time to let go of my old ways, to embrace a new path. I'll show Lily that I'm not inflexible, that I'm willing to change because she's worth it.

She's worth everything.

Chapter Thirty-Five

L^{ily}

My chest fills with warmth as I read the text again. I've pulled it out and looked at it so many times, though I haven't been able to give Ethan a meeting time yet.

I have unfinished business, and I just completed one piece of it. I told Noah what Mason did to me.

Noah starts to pace my bedroom, his hands clenched into fists at his sides. "I'm going to kill him."

I don't even have the slightest urge to snap at him like I did so many times at Ethan when he said similar things. God, I was selfish. How would I have felt if I learned that someone close to me had done something so despicable to a person I love? I'd want to kill them too.

I tried to put a lock on Ethan's emotions because I wasn't

ready to confront my own. I've never been good at dealing with hard things. I usually seek distraction instead. Turns out, this is a pain far too deep for that. The only way to heal from this is to face it head-on.

Which is why I invited Noah over here today. It wasn't easy sharing my story for the second time. Certain details seemed to be too much for him. When I told him about how Mason called me crazy the morning after the rape, he looked ready to punch a wall. But even with Noah's volatile temper, my heart is a little lighter.

Sharing is good. It takes away the power of the secret.

"Lily..." Noah's eyes fill with pain and anger. "Why didn't you tell me? I've been living with that piece of shit. I could have moved out months ago. I could have beaten him to a pulp." He shakes his head. "You should have told me."

Irritation flares in my chest, even though I know Noah's anger isn't really directed at me. What a contrast to the way Ethan reacted though. He didn't try to make me feel guilty for keeping my secret locked away. He was all gentle steadiness, like a lighthouse guiding a ship through a storm.

"You can't let him get away with this," Noah says. "That broken nose isn't enough."

"That's actually why I invited you over. Can you arrange a meeting with Coach Rodriguez?"

Noah's eyes widen. "You're going to try to get him kicked off the team, aren't you?" A grin spreads across his face. "That would be like death to Mason. His dumb ass doesn't even know he's not that good of a quarterback. He's destined for high school coaching, not the NFL. But this could kill all his career prospects. No one wants to hire a rapist, and if we take this story to the university news center—"

I raise a hand. "One thing at a time. This isn't about punishing Mason. It's about making sure he doesn't hurt anyone again. It's also..." I take a deep breath. "Noah, I need to show Ethan how sorry I am. You heard how I raged at him after the game, and he didn't do anything wrong. I need to make sure the coach understands why he hit Mason."

Noah's grin dissolves in an instant, replaced by a scowl. "I can't believe you're worried about him. He doesn't deserve anything. He used you. And he lied to me."

It takes all my willpower to keep my eyes from rolling. My dear older brother feels so much younger than me sometimes. "Do you hear yourself? You think Ethan Harrington used me? It's about as ridiculous as Jesus opening an OnlyFans. You're just pissed off because you feel left out. We kept a secret from you. You felt like Ethan belonged to you—" I shoot him a cheeky smile "—but it turns out he really belongs to me."

Except maybe he doesn't. He never made any long-term commitment to me, but I can't think about that now.

I'll channel Ethan's mindset, putting the greater good ahead of my own selfish concerns.

Noah grimaces. "You make it sound like I want to fuck my best friend. I'm pissed off because I thought he always told the truth. Turns out I don't even know him."

"You do know him. It's because of his integrity that he kept my secret from you. I made him promise, and Ethan doesn't take his promises lightly."

It's only after the words are out that the truth of them fully hits me. Ethan only broke his promise to keep out of the situation with Mason because there was no other way. He had to protect me, because I wasn't willing to protect myself.

Noah sighs heavily. "Maybe I'm being childish. I guess I need to think more about it."

"Please do," I say firmly. "Ethan would be heartbroken if he lost your friendship."

Noah's eyelids flutter. "God, you two being so lovey-dovey is going to be annoying."

His words make my heart skitter, but I can't get ahead of myself. Ethan and I still have so much to resolve. We both said so many things in anger. Would he even want a relationship with someone who doesn't share his moral code?

I can't think about that right now. I have to deal with the situation with Mason, regardless of the outcome.

"When do you think we can meet up with Coach Rodriguez?" I ask Noah.

He pulls his phone from his pocket. "I'll text him now. If I say it has something to do with Ethan, he'll see us right away. That's his golden boy."

I nod. "Let's see him as soon as possible."

Chapter Thirty-Six

E^{than}

We're on a bus on our way to play against Redwood State. It was at a game against them last year that I first got the attention of scouts. They were there to see Redwood's cornerback. He's really good, and this is the biggest game of the season.

I don't give a shit though. Football doesn't make me happy anymore.

Not without her.

She's been fobbing me off for three fucking days. I texted her the moment I left Brandon's, ready to pour my heart out, and she said she had "unfinished business" to take care of before she could talk to me.

Unfinished business? What the fuck does that even mean? I've been aching with the need to resolve our differences since we had our big fight, even before I realized the changes I need to make within myself.

Maybe she doesn't feel the same way. Maybe the time we

spent together—soul searing and life-changing for me—was only a fling for her.

The idea alone is a physical ache in my chest. I want to spend the rest of my life with her. I don't even care that she doesn't want to get married. I'm done with my false god of chastity and meaningless rituals. I'm ready to worship her, throw myself on the altar of Lily Greenwood.

"Hey." Noah's voice cuts through my reverie. He sits down on the leather bench and scoots beside me. My pulse kicks up. He's been ignoring me ever since our fight, which was to be expected.

I sensed the surprise among our teammates when he didn't take his usual seat next to me after boarding the bus. No one was brave enough to take his place. Not after I punched one of our teammates.

I welcomed the privacy. I'm too in my head for polite conversation anyway.

"Did you see Mason's face?" Noah asks.

A smile rises to my lips. I saw Mason right before we boarded the bus, and I'm surprised Coach didn't bench him tonight. His nose is purple and blue, the skin around it puffy and discolored. He's also been avoiding eye contact with me, his usual cockiness completely gone. He's a shadow of his former arrogant self.

He deserves so much worse.

Noah chuckles. "You should see your own face right now. You look bloodthirsty. Not that I blame you."

His light mood is odd given our last conversation, but it eases the tension in my shoulders. I ought to be ecstatic that I might have my best friend back.

If only I had Lily too. Then I'd have nothing left to wish for.

I scratch the back of my head. "So I take it you had a talk with Lily...about what happened."

"Yes," he says through clenched teeth. "She told me everything."

I nod slowly. "I would have punched him weeks ago, but she

made me promise…" I flinch. "I guess I'm not as good at keeping promises as I used to think I was. As you've learned."

"Ethan… Are you talking about your chastity vow? It's really none of my business."

I shake my head. "I meant your rule that no teammates are allowed to date your sister."

He groans. "It was a stupid rule. Actually, Lily told me it was patriarchal. Her exact words were, 'Noah, you're acting like a patriarchal little bitch who would sell me for a pair of oxen a thousand years ago.'"

Laughter rumbles from my chest, and yet I somehow want to weep at the same time. Fuck, I miss her sense of humor. It would border on viciousness coming from anyone else, but she's too playful to give serious offense. It always feels like she's laughing with you, pulling you out of your own head and into her world of light and warmth.

Noah laughs along with me. "She's ridiculous. I wrote her direct quote down in my phone because it was so unhinged."

"Fuck, I love her."

Noah's laughter fades, and he falls silent. The quiet stretches on, filled only with the hum of the bus engine.

"You're heartbroken," he eventually says. "I can see it all over your face."

I sigh. "Yeah."

"I don't think you need to be. I think… I shouldn't be telling you this. Lily probably wants to be the one to tell you, but fuck it. You look too pathetic for me to keep a secret."

He laughs again, and the hairs on my arm stand up. What the hell is he going to tell me?

"Lily and I… We went to Coach Rodriguez this morning. She told him everything, and when I tell you it was like a bomb went off in his office, that's not even an exaggeration. You know Coach. He's always talking about our character and shit, and how it matters on the field. I think he's glad you punched Mason. He even said he's going to stand by you in post-game interviews, to help with your draft prospects."

My pulse quickens, and a surge of hope courses through me, making my heart swell until it feels like it's almost too big for my chest. Lily finally came forward. That was the "unfinished business" she was talking about.

My brave, sweet girl. It couldn't have been easy to share that story with Coach Rodriguez, who's practically a stranger to her. Fuck, I wish I could hold her right now.

No, I can't get ahead of myself. Just because she came forward doesn't mean she's forgiven me.

Noah pats my back. "Don't get your hopes up too high. Coach couldn't make us any promises about getting Mason kicked off the team. Ultimately, it's up to the university admin, and they've already decided not to discipline a player who punched another teammate." Noah chuckles. "But I think there's a good chance they'll make a different decision this time. Mason's no Ethan Harrington. He doesn't carry our team, and Coach is going to point out that Derek Thompson is solid and ready to step up."

I snort. "Solid is an understatement. Derek might be young, but he's got a cannon arm." I turn to Noah, softening my voice. "But what about Lily? How did she handle the whole thing?"

Noah grins. "She was amazing. She didn't go into detail about what Mason did to her, which was a blessing for me. I'm about to murder that motherfucker already, and I don't need any more fuel. But after her story was over, she was back to her usual fearless self. In fact, she told Coach if the university admin doesn't kick Mason off the team, she'll go on social media and call them a bunch of misogynistic twats. His eyes almost popped out of his head."

Warmth spreads through my chest, a sensation so powerful it almost makes me dizzy. "I wish I could have seen that," I say, smiling wide. "My sassy girl."

Noah grimaces. "Oh my God, Ethan. Don't make me throw

up. Is this going to be my life now? I'll have to sit through watching the two of you ready to jump each other?"

I whip my head in his direction. "Did she say something to you... I mean, about wanting to be with me?"

He looks like he's fighting an eye-roll. "I guess I shouldn't be surprised that you're acting like a kid in junior high. You've never had a girlfriend before. No, she didn't say anything. You need to talk to her." He smiles lazily. "But don't think I didn't notice that you don't seem at all excited that I've forgiven you. I guess I haven't outright said it yet, but I think it's pretty obvious. All you seem to care about is her. I see the state of things now."

His words are light, but I still get the sense that he's a little hurt. I set my hand on his shoulder and give it a squeeze. "You know I love you like a brother, and I'll be ecstatic that you've forgiven me once my head is clear. But right now, all I can think about is your sister. Turns out love makes me obsessed. Everything I gave to football, school, and my faith all belongs to her now."

He grunts. "Well, you'd better start thinking about football soon. Redwood State is tough. You can't afford to be distracted by Lily. You'll need every ounce of focus to break through their defense."

I groan. "I just wish I could have talked to her already. I'm going crazy wondering what she's going to say."

Noah gives me a hard pat on the back. "Think of Lily when you play tonight. Think of your future. Treat Redwood State's cornerback like he's the one thing standing between you and her."

I nod, though I'm not sure how I'll be able to detach from my thoughts of Lily, no matter how important this game is. Knowing she went to Coach Rodriguez set off a flicker of hope that's growing like a wildfire within me, making me burn to see her.

It all has to mean something. I've been pushing her from the beginning to make sure Mason faces some consequences. She must now agree that's the right thing to do, despite what she told me days ago.

I've already decided to compromise my rigid ideals for her, and to ease back on my overprotectiveness. Could she be making a similar compromise for me?

Oh God, I don't know, and I'm too scared to get my hopes up. I won't be home until late tonight, and the next several hours are going to stretch like an eternity.

Chapter Thirty-Seven

L^{ily}

"To be honest, I always thought Mason was creepy," Lorelai says before taking a sip of her wine. "He sort of has a rapey vibe—" Her eyes grow wide, and then she winces. "Shit, Lily. What an awful thing to say. It literally just came out of my mouth. I wasn't thinking about—"

I lift a hand as I fight to contain my laughter. "It's okay, love. I don't want to treat the word 'rape' like it means something shameful about me. Mason *does* have a rapey vibe because he's a rapist. He raped me." I let out a breath. "Look at me. I can say it without flinching."

Kinsley sets her hand on my back and rubs small circles. She was her usual motherly self when I told her and the girls the whole story. The first thing she did was grab me a box of tissues from the kitchen. I didn't need it, but the gesture warmed me. Even a few days ago, I would have considered it condescending, a sign that she thinks I'm weak.

What horseshit. Crying over something traumatic isn't a weakness. Quite the opposite. It's a sign that I'm willing to confront my pain, to face it head-on, rather than run from it like I have for the last six months.

Ava leans forward. "Lily, I was wondering... Did Ethan punch Mason because he knew what he did? It just seems so...coincidental, especially since you were staying with him."

I huff out a breathless laugh. "Yes. I begged him to keep my secret, to pretend like he had no idea, but it turns out the pressure got to be too much for him. I guess Mason said something gross about me after the game, and Ethan lost it."

All three girls react simultaneously. Kinsley's hand freezes mid circle on my back, and Ava's jaw drops. "Oh my God, Lily," Lorelai mutters. "That's so hot."

I grin, and warmth spreads through my veins. My beautiful, principled Ethan defended my honor. I wasn't ready to see it at first, and it might be a little antiquated, but it's kind of adorable.

He didn't do it because I'm incapable of defending myself, but because I refused to do it. I was hiding from my pain, and Ethan inadvertently forced me to confront it.

It was the right thing to do. My body and my spirit are as light and easy as they've been in months. I'll never be the old Lily again. I've learned that. But it's not a tragedy. This new Lily is stronger, braver, and ready to face the world with a renewed sense of purpose.

Standing up against Mason isn't just for me. It's also for any other woman he could have hurt. I won't let him get away with what he did. The next thing I plan to do is go to the university news center and tell my story. It's time for the truth to come out, and I'm ready to tell my story.

"Yeah," I say. "It is kind of hot."

There's a knock at the door—three quick raps. All three girls jump, their eyes wide. The door creaks open, and Ethan steps inside the house. My heart leaps into my throat.

"Oh my God," I mutter. "I conjured him."

"No, you didn't conjure me," Ethan says, his expression grim as he strides into the living room. "I called you like fifty times. Your phone went straight to voicemail."

My head swims. "I think it died."

He groans. "Typical Lily. I can barely breathe because I need to see you so badly, and you're not even sure if your phone died. You only *think* it did."

My head grows fuzzy. Why does he seem so upset?

When I examine his face, his eyes are dark and troubled. My heart clenches for him.

They must have lost the game. Noah told me it was one of the most important of Ethan's career, that it could seal his NFL potential if he performed well.

I couldn't watch it. I couldn't even look at the score, so I let my phone die on purpose. The thought that I might see Ethan's dreams shatter in a handful of numbers was unbearable.

Turns out seeing it on his face is so much worse.

"Was it a bad loss?" I ask. "I'm sure it wasn't your fault. Even if you...got tackled or...something."

He whips around to face me, his face incredulous. "We won the game, Lily. You would know that if your goddamn phone wasn't dead."

I blink in surprise. If they won, why is he being so grumpy? He should be ecstatic.

I cross my arms over my chest. "Ethan, you've outdone yourself. You're vacuuming up your own joy now. It's more impressive than winning a big game. You should get a... What is that stupid football award? A Heisenberg, or whatever."

Ethan's face contorts, and a strangled sound escapes his throat, then he bursts into laughter. His whole body shakes with it, and it echoes through the room. It's as if a dam has broken, and he can't stop.

The girls look at me with huge eyes. I can only shake my head in response. I'm just as bewildered as they are. He's almost hysterical.

Is this all for me?

"It's called the Heisman trophy," Ethan says, his voice strangled with laughter. "And they won't give it to me for vacuuming up joy, no matter how good I am at doing it."

As his laughter fades, Ethan's eyes soften. His gaze is warm and tender, and the corners of his mouth are still twitching. "I think you might be the most ridiculous person I've ever met."

The words are sweet, caressing. My heart flutters as a realization dawns within me.

Ethan accepts me exactly as I am. He finds my ridiculousness endearing, just as I find his steadfastness reassuring. We balance each other in ways I never thought possible. His strength calms my chaos, while my spontaneity brings light to his rigidity.

It's a harmony I never knew I needed.

And maybe he needs it too.

Ethan takes slow steps in my direction. "My performance is the reason we won tonight. I made a nearly impossible catch in the fourth. That's not a brag. The replay is all over the news right now. I've been sent a million videos since the game ended." He smiles faintly. "I'm probably going to get drafted."

My heart soars. "Ethan, that's wonderful. Amazing."

He shrugs. "I guess it should be, but I just can't bring myself to give a shit." His dark-blue eyes lock onto mine. "What does any of it matter if I don't have you?"

My heart swells like a flower blooming under the sun as he reaches out and grabs my chin. "I know I fucked up. I never should have punched Mason. I see that now. And I sure as hell shouldn't have stuck to my guns after I did it, but..." He licks his lips. "I'm willing to change, Lily. My strict principles are worthless if I'm miserable. And I'm miserable without you. Nothing matters. Not football. Not even God. You've become..." His voice cracks. "You've become everything to me.

My vision blurs, and I blink. My heart is about to burst.

I swallow. "You really mean it?"

"Yes," he says immediately, and the world around me sparkles with electricity.

"But...is that okay? I don't want you to feel like you're giving up who you are for me."

His lips quiver as he smiles. "I'm not giving up anything. I'm finding a new way, and God wouldn't make me give up the only joy I've ever known."

I blink away the tears filling my eyes. "And what is that?" My voice is breathless."

His throat moves unsteadily. "You. You're my love, Lily." His voice wobbles. "My true love."

I nod jerkily. "And you're mine."

His eyes grow huge. "Really?" he nearly shouts. He yanks me into his arms. His hands cradle my face, his thumbs brushing away my tears. He leans in slowly, his breath warm against my lips. The world fades away as he captures my mouth in a deep, passionate kiss. His lips are soft but demanding, moving against mine with a desperate urgency. I melt into him, my hands clutching his shirt as if letting go would mean losing him forever.

Applause erupts around us, pulling me into the present world. We pull apart, breathless and laughing. Ethan's forehead rests against mine, a smile spreading across his face. "You could have offered to take me into your bedroom so we didn't have an audience."

I shoot him a saucy smile. "I could have, but then my girls would have missed the show." I pinch his cheek. "Plus, you know how much I enjoy torturing you."

He narrows his eyes. "Sassy girl."

"Get used to it, big guy. This is only the beginning."

L^{ily}

Ethan is nibbling on my neck, his hand grazing over my chest, cupping my breast with gentle possession. A tired groan escapes my chest. "I can't," I whimper. "I'm too tired."

"Sorry, love," he whispers into the dark of my bedroom. The mattress shifts as he pulls away. "I'll stop, I promise." There's a pause, and his breath is hot against my ear. "Just one last kiss?"

My heart grows light as air. How did my life change so much in the span of a month? Just last week, Mason was finally held accountable. First, he was kicked off the Hawks, and yesterday, the full truth finally came out to the whole campus. My interview about the rape was published in the campus newspaper.

The very evening it was released, a girl DMed me. She didn't say much, but she told me she had her own story about Mason to share. She asked me to meet with her and said she thought I was the only person in the world who could understand.

My heart swelled with a mixture of relief and sorrow. If only I had shared my story sooner. But at least I did. I finally let go of my longing for the old Lily so that I could become a version of her who's resilient.

And now here I am. Ready to drift off to sleep in the bedroom that once filled me with restless dread. The only thing left to do is turnaround my grades, but it no longer feels so daunting. Resilient Lily can take on any obstacle, all because of this wonderful man who taught her that pain can't be run from. It only leads to more pain.

"Okay, one more kiss," I whisper.

In a flash, he's on top of me again. His kiss starts slow and soft, but then it grows more passionate. Hungry.

His hips grind against mine. The touch of his thumb against my nipple sends a jolt through me, and I'm pulled out of my dreamy haze.

When his hand slips between my legs, I giggle. "This definitely escalated beyond a simple goodnight kiss."

Ethan rolls off me, and the moonlight from the window casts a soft glow on the sharp angles of his face. "I guess I got carried away. You're too delicious."

"Alright, fine." I smile. "Now that I'm awake, you might as well wear me out with another round."

"Are you sure?"

I snort. "Yes, big guy."

"Prepare yourself," he says huskily. "You don't have to do any work, but I want to feel every perfect inch of this pussy." He pokes his finger inside me. "It belongs to me now."

I snort at his possessive words. How strange that they don't make me feel the slightest bit caged. He owns me because I gave myself to him freely. And I own him.

I trace the line of his jaw, and warmth surges through me like an unstoppable tide. He's my missing piece.

His brow furrows. "What are you thinking about?"

"I think I want to marry you someday," I whisper.

Ethan's body stills, and his eyes grow wide. Then, as if understanding dawns, his expression transforms. Happiness blooms across his features, as radiant as the sun sparkling on the ocean.

"Really?" The question is breathless.

"Really."

"But I thought... I'm okay if you never want to get married."

I sigh. "I know, but I changed my mind."

He narrows his eyes, looking so adorably skeptical I want to laugh. "How could you change your mind that quickly about something so huge?"

I smile. "You're learning the difference between me and you. You're devoted to your principles and opinions, and I'm a slut with mine. My plan to never get married no longer serves me. Not when I've found the love of my life. So it's gone."

"Just like that?"

"Just like that."

Ethan bursts into laughter, his chest vibrating against mine.

I frown. "I'm sorry? I just told you I wanted to marry you, and you're laughing?"

His chuckles fade as he stares at me with hooded eyes. He runs his fingers through the hair behind my ear. "I was just thinking I kept my virginity pledge after all." His eyes twinkle. "I did lose my virginity to my future wife."

I laugh, and the sound bubbles from deep within me and echoes through the room.

"It doesn't matter, though," he says. "I would have 'lived in sin,' as Christian's say, for the rest of my life if it meant keeping you." His expression grows serious. "I might be moving out of state at the end of the year, so we'll need to make a plan. If I make it to the NFL, I'll have plenty of money to fly you out to see me. We can do it monthly, and we'll have plenty of FaceTime dates and—"

I silence him with a kiss. "Relax, lord and master. You don't have to plan out my entire life in one night. You're making me tired again."

He grins. "Then I guess I'll have to wake you up."

And he does.

He loves me slowly and tenderly, with all the patience of a man who adores me flaws and all. His touch is deliberate, worshipful, as if he's memorizing the feel of my skin under his fingertips. The steady rhythm of our bodies moving together lulls me into a state of half-conscious bliss.

I called it "another round" earlier. What an understatement.

This is the beginning of forever.

Thank you for reading! Want more Ethan and Lily right now? Sign up for my newsletter by using the link below, and you'll get a FREE spicy second epilogue!

www.skylermason.com/sin

Untitled Skyler Mason project...

What happens when the leader of a pleasure cult tries to seduce the pastor's daughter?

Untitled Skyler Mason Project

Author Note

Who do you think fell first, Ethan or Lily? Go to my Facebook group and tell me your answer. I'm very active in this group and will respond to your comment as soon as I can.

Mason's Minxes on Facebook

Acknowledgments

My dearest Gabrielle Sands, thank you for always being there for me and helping me grow as an author.

Claire Taylor, I could not have finished this book without you. You helped me learn my characters and, more importantly, myself.

My editor Heidi Shoham, thank you for always pushing me to be a better writer.

Becca Mysoor, thank you for brainstorming with me and making this book sparkle.

Mazzi, thank you for your thorough beta read. You gave me the confidence to finally hit publish.

My dearest PA Tiffany, thank for proofreading this book and being my brain whenever mine goes missing.

To my readers, I love you. Without you, these stories in my head would never make it to the page.

Also by Skyler Mason

The Purity Series

Purity

Shame

Lust

Sin

The Faithless Duet

Faithless

Forgiveness

The Toxic Love Series

Wild and Bright

Revenge Cake